CURVY GIRLS CAN'T DATE CURVY GIRLS

KELSIE STELTING

*This book is for love, for joy,
for being yourself out loud.*

CONTENTS

ONE

XIOMARA

PEOPLE like me were supposed to hate school assemblies.

I should have detested cheerleaders and their short skirts that were surely designed with the patriarchy in mind.

But I couldn't find it in me to be bothered. Not with the cute way Kiyana's cheer skirt fluttered around her thighs. Not with the way her sparkly blue eyeshadow only drew more attention to her pretty, dark eyes. And definitely not with the smile she wore as she sang and danced to the Emerson Academy fight song.

A preppy, curvy girly girl like Kiyana would never go for someone like me. Heavy, as clumsy as they came, and two years younger. Especially not when she was dating the school's star quarterback and had been for the last four years.

"What do you think, Xi?" Van asked. I looked over to my best guy friend, who was holding hands with his girlfriend, Ronnie.

"About what?" I asked.

On my left, Shelley smirked. "She was too busy paying attention to the cheerleaders to hear you."

"As if," I lied.

Van wore a knowing grin and said, "I was asking if you wanted to go to Waldo's tonight. Celebrate the end of our imprisonment. At least for the summer."

I laughed. "A milkshake does sound good. Even if it will be super crowded."

Shelley said, "Then you won't mind if Gunnar comes along?" She was already blushing, and I had to grin.

"That cute guy you've been texting?"

She nodded. "He's been wanting to hang out."

"Invite him," Van said, and Ronnie nodded her agreement. They were the only couple in our friend group, and I knew she was dying for double dates that didn't just involve Shelley and me tagging along.

The cheering ended, and our guidance counselor, Birdie Bardot, took the microphone. "It's been another great year at Emerson Academy! The football team made the playoffs. Go, Drafters!"

The football players cheered the loudest of everyone.

"Our school production of *Annie* was incredible!"

More cheering from the drama kids.

"The marching band performed at the Badgers halftime show!"

Even louder cheering that now included some blaring instruments.

"And we have so much to look forward to, like Emerson Academy participating in Emerson's first pride celebration with an inclusive prom!"

The clapping was noticeably quieter, and I felt the heavy weight of eyes on me. As if the rumor mill weren't enough to let everyone in school know that I liked girls, my mom was the very public head of the Emerson Pride Association and the bank where my dad worked had funded many educational sessions on inclusion at our school.

I was as out as out could be—with the notable exception of a girlfriend or anyone even close.

"We're dismissing everyone to clean up their lockers, and then you are free to go and enjoy your summer! Be sure to pick up a flyer for the inclusive prom during Emerson's pride celebration and your summer reading list on your way out!"

The shuffle of students began around us, and I followed my friends along the bleachers and out of the gym. There were fifty-four kids in our class, but I probably wouldn't see most of them over the summer. These four were my people, and I was glad to have them.

We parted ways to go to our lockers, and Van called, "See you at Waldo's. Five thirty, okay?"

Shelley and I exchanged a glance. "That means eight," I said, sticking my tongue out at Van. He could have worn all the watches in existence and still wouldn't be on time.

"Ha ha," he said and turned to walk away, his hand linked with Ronnie's.

Shelley glanced at me and said, "See you later, Xi."

I lifted my fingers in a wave and went down the hallway that had my locker. It was at the end of the sophomore hall, which luckily gave me plenty of room to begin clearing it out, starting with pulling down photos of my friends and a mini poster of the Indigo Girls.

I carefully slid them into a folder and then got to work taking out my books. I always kept my favorites on hand because I never knew when there would be free time to read. The problem with having so many books? Having to carry them home. (Or at least to my mom's car, where she'd be waiting in the parking lot.)

I filled my backpack to the point of bursting and still had several left. So I stacked them carefully, holding them in my arms and using my chin to hold them in place.

Using my hip, I bumped my locker door, but the janky thing never closed unless you lifted up on the lock and slid it shut.

"Crap," I muttered, not wanting to set my books on the floor and start all over.

"Here, I'll help you," a beautiful, clear voice said.

My eyes widened and I nearly dropped all my books when I realized who had spoken. Kiyana was standing in front of me, offering to help.

She pushed on the door, but just like always, it caught. "Is it broken?" she asked.

Finding my voice, I said, "You have to lift up on the hinges."

She wrapped her fingertips around the underside of the lock and pushed, using her hip to secure it. "They should really fix that," she said.

"Tell me about it. I told them about it at the beginning of the year."

She laughed. "Figures."

I glanced around, wondering where her boyfriend was, where her usual posse of cheerleaders had gone. But instead of answering my silent question, she said, "Do you need help carrying those outside?"

I hesitated. This had been the extent of our conversation for my two years in high school with her... despite how often I'd looked her way when she wouldn't notice. It felt too good to be true. "Are you sure?"

"Anything to keep from turning in my pom poms." She grabbed half the stack from me. Now that I looked away from her beautiful dark eyes, I realized she was wearing leggings and a long T-shirt.

"They make you turn them in right away?"

She nodded, walking beside me toward the exit. "I would steal mine if I could." She laughed. "I'm going to miss cheering here."

"But you're cheering in college, right?" I asked

and instantly blushed. I shouldn't have known that. Shouldn't have cared enough to remember.

If it bothered her, she didn't let on. "Yeah. I actually leave in a few weeks to start training."

"Three weeks?" I did the math in my head. The inclusive prom was three weeks from now. If time was on my side, we could go togeth—

I quickly shut down that thought. It didn't do me any good to fantasize about girls I could never have. Girls who would never be interested in me in a million and one years.

"We have cheer camp for a week so the squad can get to know each other, and then we start practicing for the football season. It'll be so much fun. And so different."

We reached the front doors of the school, and someone held the door open for us. Or, let's be real, for Kiyana. She was Emerson Academy royalty. Literally. She'd been homecoming queen, and I'd voted for her.

We slowly went down the steps, and she asked, "Where are you parked?"

My cheeks felt hot in a way that had nothing to do with the early summer sun. "My mom's waiting for me over there." I nodded toward her maroon sedan that I *hoped* would be mine someday.

"Great," she replied. We got closer to the car and stopped. "You know," she said, "I never told you how much I admired you. For coming out this year. It was really brave of you." There was something behind her smile. Something I didn't understand, but it didn't feel malicious.

"Thanks?" I said awkwardly because... well... that's who I am.

She nodded, and I heard the car door open as Mom got out. Mom took the books from Kiyana, and we filled the trunk. When I looked up to thank her, Kiyana was already walking away.

"That was nice of her," Mom said.

I nodded, looking after the girl who had been my biggest crush for the last two years and thinking I wanted so much more than for her to be proud of me.

TWO

KIYANA

I SET my pom poms on the table in front of Coach Alexander. Lots of people didn't like her, but I was thankful for her. She'd taken a chance on me as a plus-size cheerleader. Made me an invaluable part of our stunt routines. And ultimately, made me good enough to cheer at Elmbrooke University. (Thanks in part to the fact that they were one of the few local colleges without a weight limit in order to be on the cheer team.)

"How's it feel?" Coach asked.

"My eyes are sweaty," I said with a strangled laugh as I gave my blue and silver pom poms one last look. I'd spent so much time with them the last four years I could remember exactly the way my hands felt around the hard handles, the shimmery plastic moving against my skin.

She nodded. "You've been a solid part of the team, Kiyana. I think you'll make a great cheer coach one day."

It was high praise. Especially from a woman who didn't dole out compliments often. "That means a lot, Coach."

"Of course." She lifted her chin. "Have a great summer."

"I will," I said. But really, I was wondering how I could get it to go by faster. My grandparents were visiting for the next month, and Stefon and I were still putting on a show. If I was being honest, going to college felt like an exhale.

It would be a place where I could be myself, without so much pretending.

A place where maybe, someday, I could go on a date with a girl like Xi.

I walked down the thinning hallways, trying not to cry. In so many ways, cheerleading had been my lifeblood—the thing to distract me from the hard parts of knowing who I really was and being unable to share it.

I knew the second I came out, everything would have changed. Things would have gotten weird in the locker room, people would have made comments at the lunch table, and don't even get me started about the abuse I'd endure in the parking lot or hallways.

I'd like to think better of my classmates, but I remembered what it was like when Xi came out. How long it took for the gossip to settle back down. How hard some parents fought to keep inclusive messages from touching our ears.

I let out a sigh as I stepped outside, alone this time. But I wouldn't be alone for long. Stefon had picked me up for school this morning, and he should be waiting for me in the parking lot by his SUV.

I walked toward his parking spot and found him sitting in the back with the hatch raised up.

"Hey," he said, not moving from his spot.

"Hey," I replied, sitting next to him with my legs dangling. I glanced around at the few cars left in the parking lot. None of them were within earshot of us. "Last day of school."

He swiveled his head toward me, squinting against the sun. "We made it."

The smile I gave felt hard-won, just like keeping our secret for the last four years.

He'd been my fake boyfriend since our first

boy/girl party freshman year when we were forced into the closet for Seven Minutes in Heaven.

As if it was happening right in front of me all over again, I could see him standing across the from me in the walk-in closet, a panicked look in his eyes. I'd been about to kiss him, just to get it over with, because I didn't want anyone to know... I'd liked girls for about a year and hadn't told a single soul. He looked genuinely terrified.

"We can just get it over with," I'd whispered quietly, trying not to feel rejected even though I hadn't wanted to kiss him either.

"I—I can't," he said, on the verge of hyperventilation.

I'd walked across the closet, rubbing his back. "I can't kiss you, because I'm... gay," he'd said.

I'd stared at him in shock. Out of all the people I'd been thrown into the closet with, he'd had the same secret as me.

"Please don't tell anyone," he'd said. "You're the only person who knows." Tears were pooling in his eyes then, worry clear on each of his features.

"You don't have to worry about me," I'd said, taking a deep breath. "I like girls."

For the rest of our four minutes in "heaven," we'd cooked up a plan. We'd be boyfriend and girlfriend for the rest of high school. He could be on the football team without things getting weird with the other players, and I could keep my preferences from my strait-laced conservative family and the girls on the cheerleading squad.

And it had worked. We'd gone to every prom, every party, every double date together. We'd even been voted homecoming king and queen. (He'd kissed me on the cheek since everyone now knew we "didn't like PDA.")

After all this time... Stefon was more than my fake boyfriend. He was my best friend.

But now everything was changing. And that scared the crap out of me.

"What if we extended our agreement, just for the summer?" I asked.

He raised his eyebrows. "What?"

"My mom's already planning our joint going-away party. And if I come out and they take it badly, I'd just be stuck in the house with them all summer. It sounds like literal hell."

He took a breath, his shoulders rising and falling. "You don't want to start dating? See who's out there? I know there are apps—maybe we can meet someone from LA or even Elmbrooke?"

"You want to start dating?" I asked, stunned.

He reached over and held my hand. It felt just as brotherly as ever. "The last four years have been great, doing everything with my best friend, but I'm tired of putting that part of my life on hold. I want to see what's out there."

Fear scrabbled at my stomach. Because if Stefon stopped being my boyfriend, if he started dating boys, that would only lead to questions from my parents.

Questions I wasn't ready to answer.

"Please, Stef. Just a few more weeks."

He hesitated.

My stomach sank. "*Please*. You can date someone else, meet someone else. But please don't tell our parents yet. Not until we're leaving, okay?"

He let out a sigh, then nodded. "For you."

A corner of my lip twitched into an echo of a smile. I had a deadline. But I knew, when it came time, I still wouldn't be ready.

"Come on," he said, getting out of the trunk. "Let's go get some ice cream."

THREE

XIOMARA

WALDO'S DINER was just as crowded as I thought it would be. My friends and I shouldered past all the people walking out and scanned the diner for an open booth that would seat the five of us.

That's right. Five.

As in, I was the fifth wheel, and everyone else was coupled up.

Usually I didn't mind being single, but times like these, I really wished I had someone. If only so I didn't get stuck sitting in a chair at the end of the table while the others cuddled up next to each other and held hands.

I wished I could have someone there with me to at least take up another seat. But there we were, sliding into a booth and borrowing a chair from another table so I'd have somewhere to sit. It didn't help that my size meant I was halfway in the aisle and constantly apologizing to people walking by.

I apologized to another person and then turned back to my friends. Ronnie held out her phone with a picture of a girl on the screen and said, "What do you think of her?"

I raised my eyebrows. "That she's blond?"

"And pretty, right?" she said.

Now I was getting suspicious. "Why?"

"We made you a dating profile. I filtered it to only people who say they're eighteen or younger."

I reached out and pushed her phone down to the table. "No."

"Why?" Shelley asked.

I glanced toward Gunnar, the guy she had brought along. I didn't really know him, but I guess it was time for his initiation. "I'm only sixteen. It's okay that I haven't dated anyone yet." That was a lie though. I *did* want to date someone, but that was something my abuela would say. *There's plenty of time for romance,* she always told me. *You're only young once.*

Which reminded me. I needed to call her to plan my summer visit.

Van said, "It's okay, but don't you want to have a date for prom?"

Definitely. I shrugged. "Maybe I'll meet someone at the pride parade or the festival."

Shelley turned to Gunnar. "Is there anyone Xi could meet at your school?"

I glared at her, and Van burst out laughing.

"Yeah, Gunnar, know any lesbians?" Van said.

Shelley blushed. "Forget I said anything."

Gunnar stared very pointedly at his drink, but he did say, "I went to prom alone this year, and it was okay."

"See?" I said, gesturing toward him. "Thank you, Gunnar." Someone ran into the back of my chair, and I nearly spilled my drink, letting out a loud, "Oof."

"Oh my gosh, I'm so sorry," Stefon, king of our high school, said. But I wasn't looking at him. I was seeing the girl behind him with the most beautiful brown eyes widened in shock.

"Are you okay, Xi?" she asked.

"Wait," Van said. "You know her name?"

We both glared at him, and I turned back to Kiyana. Toward her concerned expression. "I'm okay."

She looked like she wanted to say more, but someone was waiting behind her. She nodded and then walked behind Stefon to a long table at the back with the rest of the popular kids from our school.

My gaze must have followed her a little longer than normal because Ronnie said, "Now we know why you're not into blonds."

Van waggled his eyebrows, and I shoved his shoulder.

Shelley said to Gunnar, "Yes, they're always like this."

And to be fair, I wouldn't have it any other way.

When I got home from school, Birdie Bardot was sitting at the kitchen table with my parents. They were so engrossed in whatever they were doing, they hadn't even heard the door open. I dropped my purse loudly on the ground and raised my eyebrows. "What's going on?"

They turned toward me as if coming out of a trance, and Mom smiled, waving me over. "*Hola, bonita.* We were just looking at decorations for the prom! We need to get our order in by tomorrow for everything to make it in on time."

I walked closer to the table, and Dad made room for me to see the magazine. "Why aren't we using the internet like regular people?"

Birdie laughed. "We get a discount from this vendor."

Mom nodded. "We're going for an Under the Sea theme, so young people can enjoy it and older people can relive the proms they missed. What do you think?"

It was thoughtful actually, and I couldn't get the thought of Kiyana in a sea-green dress out of my head. But what I really said was, "It's nice. But we can't have real fish. People will go nuts."

"Good point," Birdie said, retrieving a pencil from behind her ear and writing it down in the margin of the magazine. "What do you think of these for centerpieces then?"

She flipped to another page that showed fish-bowls filled with gel-like water, castles, aquarium rocks, and plastic fish.

"I like it," I said.

"Ooh," Mom said. "We could do these to hang with the disco ball!" She pointed at jellyfish with crepe paper tendrils swirling down.

"Love it!" Birdie sang. "I think that's everything on my list."

"The only thing we have left is my dress," I said.

Mom gave me a knowing smile. "Why don't you check your room?"

My lips parted. "No way! It came in while I was at Waldo's?"

She nodded, but I was already running toward the stairs and up to my room. Shoving the door open, I could see the most beautiful dress I'd ever laid eyes on.

It was lime green, with a beaded top and a full tulle skirt that cascaded all the way to the floor.

I picked it up and held it to my chest, spinning in circles so the material flared around me. Was I in heaven? I had to be.

"It's beautiful," Mom said.

I glanced to see her and Birdie standing in the doorway. Mom's hands covered her heart, and Birdie had a huge smile on her face.

"You have great taste, Xi."

"Thanks," I said with a smile.

Mom nodded. "Hopefully it goes with whatever your date is wearing."

"I don't have a date," I said.

Mom had a sly smile. "Maybe not yet, but there's time."

I wanted to tell her it didn't matter whether I had a day, a week, or a year; getting Kiyana to fall in love with me would never happen. [Not in a million years.] No matter how much I wished it would.

FOUR

KIYANA

I SPENT my first week out of high school doing absolutely nothing. Well, next to nothing. There was a workout routine the cheer coach had given us to do over the summer. So, I slept in as late as I could. Worked out, lounged by the community pool, stayed up watching movies and did it all over again.

Going to Emerson Academy had been no joke. There were piles of never-ending homework, rigorous cheer practices, and then add on the social pressures of keeping a secret that could change your life if anyone ever found out.

This rest felt needed. It felt *earned*.

But Stefon and I had agreed to go out the following Friday night to keep up the charade. As I got ready, my grandparents sat in the living room with my parents, chatting while the TV played in the background. Stefon came to my house and knocked on my door as he had all those times before.

Hearing the commotion, I left my room, grabbing my purse, and saw Mom answering the door.

"Hi, Stefon!" she said, taking him into a hug. "How does it feel to be out of high school?"

He hugged her back and gave her his winning grin. "I haven't had much time to feel since I've been catching up on sleep."

Dad chuckled. "Lil miss has been doing the same thing."

Rolling my eyes, I said, "It's not a crime to sleep."

"Amen," Grandpa said.

Grandma nodded her agreement. "Kids do too much these days. They need time to just be kids."

Having heard this rant a million times before about all my extra-curricular activities, I was more than ready to go. "We're gonna be late for the movies," I said.

Grandpa waved his hand. "You two have fun. Good to see you again, Stefon."

"Bye, honey," Grandma added.

Stefon and I walked out the door holding hands, and Stefon said, "I think I'm the family favorite, which is saying something since you're an only child."

"Hey!" I hit his arm, laughing.

"How about being a rebel tonight?" he asked.

I got into the car, giving him a suspicious look as he got in on his side. "A rebel? At the movie theater?"

"We're not going to the movies." He buckled in and turned on the car.

"Then where are we going?"

"We're going to LA."

My mouth dropped open. "It's an hour away!"

"Your parents didn't give you a curfew, did they?"

"No, but—"

"Tell them we went over to Alyssa's to watch movies."

"When we're really going to..."

He had a wicked grin. "A queer bar."

My heart beat faster. "What? We're not twenty-one!"

"It's eighteen and up."

I sat back in my seat, taking it in. Realizing that

I would be going to my first queer space. "What if we're seen?"

He shrugged, still holding on to the wheel. "We'll say we got curious what it was like. No big deal."

We were silent for a moment.

"Or..." he said.

I raised my eyebrows. "Or?"

"You could tell your parents."

Why was he rushing this? "We agreed not to tell them until we left for college."

"True, but we only have two weeks until we leave," he said.

"Don't remind me," I muttered.

His phone spoke, and he glanced at the screen, following the directions downtown. He drove past a building called Moth and then entered a parking garage. It was dark and dank and looked exactly like the kind of place they'd film on the news announcing our murders.

"Are you sure you don't want to go to the movies?" I asked, looking around.

He opened his door. "It'll be fine."

Not wanting to go but not wanting to be alone in the car either, I got out and wrapped both my hands around his arm, walking at his side.

"Live a little," he said.

I looked up at him. "That's what I'm trying to do!" My heart rate only slowed when we reached the sidewalk and the safety of the streetlights. I could hear pounding music from inside the building, and the pulse of it had a strange kind of *life*.

We reached the front door and a bouncer sitting lopsided on a stool eyed us suspiciously. "ID?"

Stefon took his out of his wallet, and I pulled mine from my purse. The guy glanced suspiciously at our cards, but let us pass, and we entered into a whole new world.

There were dancers in skimpy outfits moving rhythmically on tables. Strobe lights flashed over people of every gender and identity rubbing their bodies together on the dance_floor. And even though smoking had been banned indoors for quite some time, there was a sweet cloud of smoke hovering in the air.

Stefon looked like a kid in a candy shop.

And me? I just felt plain scared.

"Wanna dance?" Stefon asked, barely audible over the music.

"I need a drink," I yelled back.

He nodded, following me toward the bar lined

with glass bottles. The bartenders were busy, but I stood there waiting, thankful for somewhere to keep my eyes. Everyone in here was young, close enough to our age, and I could feel their eyes assessing us. Trying to figure out who we were—and who we wanted.

Stefon raised his hand with a twenty, and the bartender nearest us took notice, quickly taking our orders. As I sipped my Shirley Temple, I couldn't help but wonder what to do now.

My eyes landed at a standing table near the dance floor, and I walked toward it, Stefon following a few feet behind.

"What do you think?" he asked, leaning his elbows on the tabletop.

I shook my head. "I think I want to go home."

He raised his eyebrows. "Home?"

I nodded. It was too loud. Too open. Too *visible*. I wanted to stay in my bubble where I was Kiyana, cheerleader, homecoming queen, beloved daughter. This felt dangerous. This felt real in a way I wasn't nearly ready for.

"Come on," he said. "You can't tell me there's no one here you'd want to dance with."

I scanned the dance floor, but I already knew my answer. I'd never been the kind of girl to have crushes, and if I was being honest, only one person had ever caught my eye. "Not really,"

He gazed at me knowingly. "Who is she?"

I took him in, from his shining black eyes to the light scar on his lip. If I couldn't be honest with my best friend, how would I ever be honest with my parents? I took a deep breath. "Xi."

XIOMARA

TWO WEEKS into summer vacation and I still hadn't found a date to the prom. The only thing I really had found was my favorite chair at the city pool. My friends and I arrived as soon as it opened and took our things to the line of reclining chairs by the fence.

There was an umbrella that gave shade to two of the chairs. Ronnie and Van sat there—Ronnie so she could see her e-reader in the sun and Van because he was so white, he made paper look tan. Shelley and I took the other two chairs, taking turns applying sunscreen to each other's backs and underneath shoulder straps. (One sunburn there and you learned your lesson.)

As soon as we were done, we lay on our bellies,

facing each other while Van and Ronnie did cute couple things like tickle each other and giggle.

"How's Gunnar doing?" I asked.

"Good. He's busy working for his dad's landscaping company or else he'd be here."

I smiled. She seemed so happy about that fact. Confident in it too. "He has to make money to take you out, right?" I teased.

"Or save for college, but whatever." She laughed. "Can you believe we're halfway through high school?"

"Not really," I admitted. The last two years had felt like ten to me. But now that I was out, I felt like I knew what to expect, and people knew what to expect of me. It was nice in that way.

Shelley nodded, already sleepy from the sun. "Think you'll get a job next summer?"

"Yeah. My parents made all my sisters get summer jobs after their junior year. It's easier that way with driver's licenses and everything."

"You could be a lifeguard," she said.

I glanced over the blue water toward the guy in red trunks sitting atop a tower. "Getting paid to be here could be nice."

She nodded. "I heard they get discounted popsicles too."

"They're a dollar," I said. "Why wouldn't they get them for free?"

From our right, Ronnie mumbled, "Great."

"What?" I asked, looking around.

"The cheerleaders are here."

Just as she spoke the words, my eyes fell on Kiyana and several of her friends from the cheerleading squad. They looked like they were made of glitter, their skin oiled and shining in the sun. Their hair perfectly done. Sunglasses catching any extra glare.

Kiyana looked stunning in a white bikini that showed off her curves and a wrap that she had tied around her waist, letting her bronze legs slip out the slit.

Shelley whispered, "She really is pretty."

My cheeks heated, and I stood up. "Let's get in the pool."

"Oh, okay?" Shelley said. "You coming, Van?"

He didn't answer, too absorbed in Ronnie.

I waved my hand at them and went to the edge of the pool, dipping my feet in. I'd read somewhere that the pool smell came from pee, and it had never been the same since then, but I tried not to think about it as I dangled my feet in the cool water.

"It feels so good," Shelley commented, sitting beside me.

I nodded, soaking in the feeling. Trying not to think about the fact that I could hear the cheerleaders laughing only feet from me. I hoped they weren't laughing at us.

"Hey!" Kiyana said. At least that's what I imagined. I turned my head toward her to confirm my guess and blinked. She was walking toward us. Oh my gosh, she was coming to talk to us!

"Talk to her," Shelley whispered.

"Hey," I said, sounding as awkward as I possibly could. "What's... up?"

"We're going to play volleyball, but there are only four of us and we thought you two might want to join so we can have three on three?"

"Definitely!" Shelley answered before I could say a word. "That sounds like so much fun, doesn't it, Xi?"

I... uh... Did sports in front of the girl I had a crush on sound fun? Not really. I was the least coordinated person on the face of the earth, and now I was supposed to do something that required hand-eye coordination to avoid getting hit in the face with a ball?

Shelley drew her legs out of the pool, standing

up and sending water dripping to the cement, dampening my swim shorts.

"Okay," I said, because what was I going to do now? Say no? Yeah, right.

We walked together toward the volleyball "court" that was really just a waist-deep pool with a net in the middle. Kiyana called to her friends, "They said yes!"

I could tell one of the cheerleaders, Jessica, wasn't really happy, but Tabby and Sophie seemed okay with it. The three of them went to the opposite side and Kiyana, Shelley, and I got into the water together.

Moments like these, I was thankful for my dark skin, because I did not want Kiyana to see how much I was blushing. Not just at her in her swimsuit, but because I was swimming in the same water she was swimming in. No matter how lame it sounded, this was the first time I'd come this close to touching a girl I liked.

Yeah. It did sound lame.

Anyway...

Jessica yelled, "Your serve," and threw a volleyball over the net. It landed between the three of us, and Kiyana said, "Why don't you go first, Xiomara?"

"You can call me Xi," I blurted.

Her smiled didn't disappoint. "Okay, Xi." She took the ball and tossed it my way. My only saving grace was that by some miracle I caught it.

That's where the good luck ended.

I took the ball with me toward the back of the pool and tossed it up like I'd been taught to serve in gym class. Unfortunately, I missed it all together, and it smacked back in the water, spraying chlorine in my eyes.

Jessica giggled, but the other girls shot her warning glances, and she quieted.

"It's okay," Kiyana said, giving me an encouraging smile. "You've got this."

Behind Kiyana's back, Shelley gave me two thumbs up. I could only imagine the amount of excitement I would get from her—and the amount of flack I would get from Van and Ronnie, who were now watching us play.

Great. A bigger audience.

Taking a deep breath, I held up the ball, lifted it in the air, and smacked it as hard as I could with my hand. It went up, sailing through the air, and landed smack in the back of Kiyana's head.

She let out a cry and held her head.

"Sorry, sorry, sorry," I muttered quickly. "I'm so sorry."

She shook her head, wincing. "Um, Shelley. Why don't you serve first?"

I was *never* going to live this down.

SIX

KIYANA

I LAY IN MY BED, trying to go to sleep, but every time I closed my eyes, all I could see was Xi in her cute little swim shorts that had lacy cutouts on the sides. Her olive-green tankini top that offset her deeply tanned skin. The way the sun bounced off the water and into her dark brown eyes, making them look almost amber.

A tapping sound came at my window, and my heart stalled. I'd read this story in *Hot Beat* magazine. About the girl who was murdered in her bed. As if it could save me, I pulled my blanket over my head, hoping whoever it was would have mercy on me.

(And yes, I know I'd be the first to die in a horror movie. Sue me.)

But the tapping persisted. And then there was a ding on my phone alerting me of a text message.

If my location was given away, I might as well be able to call 9-1-1. So I peeked above the covers, grabbed my phone, terrified of a text from an unknown number giving me the text-version of the super villain's monologue.

Stefon: Let me in!

I let out a relieved and annoyed breath, walking to the window, pulling back the curtains, and seeing him standing there in a T-shirt and sweatpants like he'd just gotten out of bed himself.

"What are you doing here?" I hissed, pulling the window open. "My grandparents are in the next room!"

"As if they could hear me!" he grunted as he climbed through.

"I thought you were a murderer!"

He straightened and looked around my room. "Why aren't your parents here then?"

My cheeks got hot, and I looked down.

"Were you really sitting here thinking a murderer was at your window and you decided to *hide*? How are you going to survive college?"

"Just fine if you don't scare me like that again," I retorted. "You about gave me a heart attack!"

He chuckled quietly, and I studied him closely to see what was going on. Stefon had never done this before. This was boyfriend/girlfriend stuff, and though we maintained the titles, this part of the arrangement never came around.

"Is everything okay?" I asked.

His smile was as wide as I'd ever seen it. "More than okay. Better than ever, actually."

I smiled back at him. I loved seeing him this happy—and it wasn't like he'd interrupted my sleep anyway. "What's going on?"

He took both of my hands and pulled me to my bed, and we sat atop my messy covers. The little light coming from my nightlight shined in his black eyes. "I met someone."

My mouth fell open. "What? You met someone?"

He nodded quickly.

"Who? How?"

"What, when, where?" he teased.

I shoved his shoulder. "You're holding out on me!"

He drew his lips together, biting them and then slowly releasing his smile again. "I was looking around Elmbrooke's website, and they have an

LGBTQ+ club on campus. I started looking around, and they have a private Facebook group. One guy and I started talking, and we kind of hit it off."

My lips were smiling, but my eyes were stinging. I was so happy and confused and sad and jealous all at the same time. "Tell me about him," I managed.

Smiling the entire time, Stefon began telling me about this person named Dillon. They had texted/flirted back and forth for a few days before deciding to talk on the phone. It was only meant to be a short call, but they ended up talking for hours. Stefon's parents had even walked into the room and assumed he was talking to me.

"When are you seeing him in person?"

Stefon looked guilty.

"What?"

"I already have."

My mouth fell open. "What! I thought you were just talking."

"We were, but I told my parents I needed to go to LA to get something for college, and instead Dillon and I met... Ki, I had my first kiss."

My throat got tight, and tears were seconds from spilling. "I'm so happy for you."

He tilted his head. "Is that why you look like you're about to cry?"

I shook my head, wiping at my eyes. "It's because I want that too."

He hugged me tight. "Your turn is coming, Ki. Just wait and see."

SEVEN

XIOMARA

OUR HOUSE LOOKED like a rainbow threw up on it. Mom had hung not one but two rainbow garden flags on our front porch that faced Emerson's Main Street. All of the windows had brightly colored semi-circle flags, and she'd even used multiple sidewalk chalk colors to write a message on the three steps leading to our front door.

LOVE

IS

LOVE

If it wasn't so completely over the top, I'd be a little more grateful, a little less embarrassed. Ever since coming out my freshman year, my parents and three older sisters had done everything they could to become allies.

On Friday movie nights, we watched LGBT romance. We never shopped at Hobby Lobby or ate at Chick Fil A. There was always a rainbow accessory on Mom's person, from a rainbow purse to little rainbow earrings she liked to wear.

Mom had even founded the Emerson Pride Association, where queer people and their allies came together to support the queer community. This year, we were having Emerson's very first pride celebration, including a parade that would go right past our house and an inclusive prom at Emerson Academy.

I'd just finished decorating for the pride prom with my guidance counselor, Birdie Bardot, and a few of my friends who had stayed my friends after I came out last year.

I had to admit, I was lucky. Luckier than a lot of my online friends who'd been kicked out of their homes or even emotionally and physically abused by their parents for their choices. But sometimes I wanted to be just me.

A regular kid.

I pushed open the front door with a massive rainbow wreath on it and walked inside. Dad was on the couch, watching a TV show. He gave me a grin and said, "Hey, Xi. How's it going?"

"Good," I said, going to give him a hug.

He kissed me on the cheek and said, "Your mom has a surprise in your room."

At the mischievous smile on his face, I cringed. "A good surprise?"

He chuckled. "Why don't you go find out?"

I gave him a playful glare and dropped my bag beside the couch before going up the creaking stairs. We lived in a hundred-year-old house that was both beautiful and had quirks, like the original interior knobs that didn't actually latch and the occasional cracks in the plaster that contractors swore were no big deal.

At the top of the stairs, I turned right and walked down the hall to my bedroom. I stepped through the door, half expecting to see my room completely redecorated in a leprechaun-approved theme, but instead found a pair of rainbow chaps on my bed.

I stared at them, mouth open in horror, wondering if my mother *actually* expected me to wear these.

"What do you think?" she asked from behind me.

I turned to see her standing in the doorway, arms folded across her chest. She was smiling hopefully, her hair in its usual bun trapped by a claw clip and wearing her uniform of an oversized T-shirt and leggings.

"What are these?" I asked, afraid to even touch the chaps. (What if she had gotten them used?)

Mom grinned so big. "They're for the prom chaperones. Get it? *Chaps* for the *chap*erones?"

I let out a horrified laugh. "The chaperones? Plural? That means more than one person will be wearing *these*?"

"Your dad will be." She giggled. "Both before and after the prom."

" *Ay Dios mío.* " My cheeks had to be bright red by now.

"Just teasing," she replied, coming to gather the chaps. "Don't worry, it'll be fun. I'm sure these will be the tamest of the outfits at prom."

I glanced at my lime-green, sparkling gown. I'd hung it by my closet so I could look at it any time I chose. She might not be wrong. "I will be getting photographic evidence," I warned.

"I'm counting on it," she said. Which was fine for her, but for my banker dad, who rarely dressed in anything but slacks, button downs, and a blazer with his enamel rainbow pin... I could only imagine.

"Will Dee be home for the prom?" I asked.

Mom nodded. "Her flight is set to land about an hour before, so she'll get here just in time. I'm still bummed Luci and Dani couldn't make it back."

"They're busy with work," I reminded her with a shrug. Mom had a hard time with my sisters moving out, going to college, getting jobs and houses of their own. I was pretty sure she'd never forgive the twins for starting their indie music store on the east coast instead of here in Emerson.

"I hope they hire an assistant soon. That's so much work for the two of them, no days off." Mom had that look in her eyes that told me she could go into full-mom-worry mode for hours, but instead, she said, "How were the decorations?"

"I think you did a better job here," I replied.

She smiled with pride. "I'm sure you did great. Birdie was made for this kind of thing."

I laughed. Our school guidance counselor and one of Mom's new best friends was definitely quirky with her unending supply of colorful dresses and earrings. "Her husband and stepson came to help with some of the heavy lifting."

"I knew Cohen would be there, but I didn't

think Ollie would be back from LA until tomorrow." She smiled, holding the chaps to her chest. "I'm excited to see them at the parade. How did the Academy's float look?"

"Like some fancy donor paid way too much to have it done."

She grinned. "Great. You're going to be so pretty on the back of the float."

Pretty and me didn't exactly go in the same sentence. While my mom was petite and had curves in all the right places, I'd gotten my father's square build, with broad shoulders and enough meat on my bones to size me out of most department stores. Not that I minded being not pretty. There were so many more important things in life.

Being *me* was more than enough.

"Maybe you'll meet someone to go to prom with next year," Mom continued.

I glanced inadvertently toward my dress. Maybe a part of me had hoped to have a date, but no one else was out at my school, and internet dating didn't sound fun to me.

"Maybe," I said, knowing that the odds of me staying single for the rest of high school and beyond were way more likely than me finding someone I already knew to go with to prom.

EIGHT

KIYANA

ON FRIDAY NIGHT, Stefon and I sat side by side at a giant table in the back room of La Belle, surrounded by friends and family. Our parents had reserved the restaurant for our going-away dinner to say goodbye before we went away to college together on Sunday as a "couple." But if Stefon stayed true to his word, those hopes would be dashed tonight.

There were already bowls of buttery garlic bread being shared around to the low hum of conversation passed easily between our families. They didn't know everything was going to change tonight.

"Are you getting so excited to go cheer?" my aunt Emily asked beside me.

I smiled and nodded. "I've had so much fun at Emerson."

"I think going to a private college was just the right decision for you," Aunt Emily said. "Not too big. You two will make lots of great friends there, especially with Stefon on the football team."

"Definitely." The truth was Elmbrooke University was the only school with a cheer team that didn't have a weight limit. I was too big to get on a D1 cheer team, but I wanted to continue doing what I love. Stefon had gotten onto the football team there with ease. He could have played at a bigger college, but he wanted to be with me. And I wanted to be with him. Even if we weren't in love, we were best friends.

I glanced to my left to see Stefon talking with his cousin Bart on the other side. Bart had played in the state championship twenty years ago and had never moved on.

Stefon didn't seem to mind. He was always good at putting on an act when everyone was around, a mask. Sometimes I couldn't believe I was the only one who saw it. But then again, I'd been wearing a mask of my own. And we've been keeping a secret that no one knows.

Was that secret really being shared tonight?

Servers brought more food to the table, plates of pasta and salad and dishes with chicken, shrimp, and steak. The smell was almost intoxicating.

I was so focused on my food I almost didn't notice how quiet it had gotten. But Emily nudged my arm, and I glanced over to see Stefon standing, his face paler than I'd ever seen it.

"Stef?" I whispered.

He glanced down at me, but only for a moment. He squared his shoulders. Fixed his blazer. And said, "I have something to say."

My lips parted and my stomach sank, immediately imagining the worst was yet to come. *Don't do it, Stef. Please don't do it.*

He either couldn't hear my silent plea or ignored it because he said, "I'm glad you all are here, because there's something I've needed to say for a long time now."

Stefon.

Aunt Emily whispered, "Are you pregnant?" but everyone ignored her, hanging on to Stefon's every word.

"I'm gay. I've known for a while, and of course, this has nothing to do with Kiyana." He glanced at me, a gentle look in his eyes. He was giving me an out, letting me carry on with my secret if I chose. "I know it might be hard for you to understand, but I wanted you to know the truth before I leave. I hope you know I'm still the same Stefon. But if you can't accept that, please just... be kind."

I should have been looking at Stefon's parents to see how they'd react, if they'd accept him. But instead I looked at my parents. At my mom's slack mouth and the shock in her eyes. At my dad, who'd gone stone-faced. At my grandparents who were shaking their heads and getting up from the table... leaving the restaurant. Walking away from a boy who had been at every birthday party, every Christmas, for the last four years. Was it really that easy for them to just walk away?

The door shut behind them, and I turned to look at Stefon's family. They were quiet. Mostly. His mom had tears streaming down her cheeks, and his dad was comforting her. Why weren't they comforting him?

He was standing at the head of the table, *alone*.

I stood up and wrapped my arms around him, hugging him just like I had in that closet all those years ago.

He had been scared then, but he'd been brave today. Braver than I had ever been. He held me tight as if I was all that was left to hang on to. That was fine. I'd be here for him, no matter what. Even if he couldn't be my fake boyfriend anymore.

He pulled back, and I looked into his eyes to see them red and teary. I looked from him to his parents, who were still sitting there in their own world.

"Are you going to say something?" I demanded of them.

"*Kiyana*," my mom admonished.

But I ignored her.

"Your son just told you the biggest news of his life. Say something!"

His parents looked up at me, as if I'd shocked them out of their pity party.

Stefon squeezed my hand. I felt like we were both holding each other up.

His dad cleared his throat and said, "Let's discuss this at home." He stood, walking Stefon's mom toward the door and gestured for Stefon to follow.

I held on to his hand, but he shook his head, signaling that he needed to go. He wanted to go.

"Call me?" I said.

He nodded.

When they were out of the room, Aunt Emily picked up her silverware and said, "Better start eating. I don't want all this food to go to waste."

As if I could eat in a moment like this.

XIOMARA

"WAKEY WAKEY, EGGS AND BAKEY!" Mom called up the stairs.

I smiled at the greeting. She always said that, even though we had cereal most days.

Even though it was still early, I could feel the buzz of the pride parade in the air. It was starting at noon, and I had to admit I was excited to ride on the Emerson Academy float. Excited to be surrounded by people like me.

We couldn't tell for sure, but we estimated that a thousand people would be in attendance from the surrounding areas, including a few groups based in LA. More than fifty people had RSVP'd to the prom. Maybe I *would* meet someone in time for prom.

I walked down the stairs into the kitchen/dining room, and my jaw dropped open. "DEE!" I ran to my big sister, nearly knocking her over with a hug. She held me back, giggling as we rocked back and forth.

"*Te extrañe*," I said. *I missed you.*

"Yo también," she said. *Me too.*

"You're early!" I stepped back, taking her in more fully and admiring the green strip at the ends of her hair. "This looks so cool," I said, taking the colored strands in my hands. "Mama, can I do this?"

Mom said, "If you pay for it."

Fair enough.

I glanced at the table and saw there were actually eggs and bacon, and Dad stood at the counter making pancakes on a griddle. "So you make special food for Dee?" I teased.

Dad waved his spatula. "Have to give her a reason to come home more often."

"You know my internship keeps me busy," Dee said. She'd been working in an animal science lab at Kansas State University, researching the effects of different feed on dairy cattle. It was different than any of us ever expected, but she seemed right at home there.

"Sit, sit," Mom said, and we followed her instructions, pulling out our usual chairs at the table. Even though most of my sisters had moved out, we still had six chairs around the table, and we always sat in the same spots. "Tell us about this boy you met."

I raised my eyebrows. "You met a boy? I thought we were in the no-dating club together."

Dee laughed, her eyes squinting as she did. "It wasn't intentional, but he's been teaching me to drive a little tractor to help clean up the pens, and he's really nice."

"You're driving a tractor?" I asked. "You didn't even pass driver's ed the first time!"

Dee glared at me. "That teacher didn't like me, and you know it."

"Probably for fear of her life," I teased.

She rolled her eyes and began filling a plate with cheesy scrambled eggs. I did the same, grabbing a few pieces of bacon as well.

Dad set a plate with a stack of pancakes on the table and said, "He sounds nice. What's his name?"

"Hernando," Dee said. "But everyone calls him Nando."

Mom smiled, crossing her fingers under her chin. "Any pictures?"

Dee's cheeks flushed pink. "Maybe."

Mom wiggled her fingers. "Gimme."

I laughed. Mom was the excited best friend everyone needed.

Begrudgingly, Dee got out her phone and tapped through to a social media profile. She enlarged a photo of him, and Mom, Dad, and I leaned in to see. He was wearing jeans, boots, and a fleece half-zip jacket, standing in front of a black and white spotted cow. He wasn't smiling, but his lips turned up slightly at the corners, and his honey-brown eyes looked kind enough.

"Can he dance?" Mom asked.

Dee and I both looked at her.

"What does that matter?" I asked at the same time Dee said, "He taught me how to two-step."

Dad chuckled, going back to the griddle. "Seems like your education is going well beyond school and your internship. I approve."

And maybe I did too, but I was still feeling a little jaded. Now that Dee was dating someone, I was the only Muñoz sister without a relationship. My absence of a prom date felt more *prom*inent than ever. (Mom would *definitely* approve of that pun.)

"So, what time do the festivities start today?"

Dee asked, artfully changing the subject away from her and Nando.

Mom could have talked about the pride celebration for hours. "I'm leaving in an hour to start set-up for the parade, which begins at noon. Xi's riding in the Emerson Academy float with Birdie's stepson, Ollie, then there's going to be a festival-type setup at Emerson Trails. A bouncy house and slide for the kids, lots of vendors set up, and fun games for everyone. The inclusive prom starts at seven, and of course you're welcome to go. I steamed your senior prom dress if you want to wear that."

"So fun!" Dee said. "It's going to be a full day."

Dad nodded. "I got off easy just chaperoning and running a table for the bank. Your mother has been amazing helping set it all up."

What was I? Chopped liver? I'd spent all of my Friday decorating the gym.

Mom waved her hand at him. "I'm happy to do it for Xi. It's like you get a second birthday, but this time the whole town is celebrating."

"Let's hope the whole town is celebrating," I said. I'd been trying not to think about how I'd react if there were protestors at the parade or the prom. I knew the school's board of trustees hadn't been a hundred percent on-board to have a float or a prom, but since all the costs came from donors, they hadn't had much of a reason to back out.

Dad rubbed my shoulder as he sat next to me. "There will always be someone out there trying to tear you down. Keep your eyes, and ears, on the people lifting you up."

I nodded, trying to internalize the advice he so often gave. It was hard sometimes, though, when you knew there were people out there who hated everything that you were.

"Plus, we have great security," Mom reminded me. "All of the EPD and EFD will be there, plus Brentwood is sending in some backup officers."

That did make me feel better, if only a little bit.

"Will anyone from school be there?" Dee asked.

I shrugged. "Van, Ronnie, and Shelly will be there, but other than that, I have no idea."

Mom glanced at the clock and smiled at us. "It's showtime."

TEN

KIYANA

MOM AND DAD hadn't said much on the way home from La Belle. Mom mentioned how much harder things would be for Stefon, Dad made a dumb joke about me "turning him gay," and that was that. It would have been easy, with just the three of us in the car, to tell them. But something held me back. It was like if I never told them, we could still be the family we'd always been.

When we got back to the house, I went to my room, turned on my TV and waited up past midnight to hear from Stefon, hoping he'd call or even tap on my window again, but he hadn't so much as texted me. With my eyelids growing heavy, I sent him a message saying to call me if he needed to talk, turned my phone on loud, and fell asleep.

My phone did ring, but not until the next morning.

I got up, rubbing my eyes, and swiped to answer. "Stefon? Are you okay?"

"I think so. Can you meet me at Halfway Café?"

"Of course. I'll be there in half an hour." I hung up and hurried to get ready, getting dressed and doing my hair in record time. I grabbed my purse and went downstairs where my parents were passing time with my grandparents in the living room. Grandpa was reading a newspaper—like a real, big newspaper with crackling paper. Grandma was knitting from balls of yarn in her purse. Dad and Mom were sitting across from each other at the coffee table, playing a game of chess.

"Where are you heading?" Mom asked as I reached the door.

"Going to meet the girls at Halfway Café," I said.

I thought that was it, but she kept talking. "That's good, you getting support. You and Stefon have been together such a long time. I can't imagine what it would feel like to break up right before going to college together."

I paused, my hand on the doorknob. I'd spent so

much time acting like Stefon and I were dating that I never imagined how to act when we broke up. "It's been rough," I said, not facing her until I could compose my features and not give away a lie. When I did, her hands were off the chess board, and she was giving me a concerned look. "Just be sure to stay clear of that pride parade. Stefon will probably be there today."

My chest felt tight, making it difficult to breathe. "Sure. See you later."

I walked out the door into the summer heat, immediately feeling better. I'd been so used to hiding around my parents, but with Stefon coming out... it made me feel more vulnerable. I didn't have the cover of a relationship anymore. And I wouldn't when we went to college either.

What would it be like to have a guy ask me out and not be able to say, "Sorry I have a boyfriend?"

Would I be able to ask girls out? Would people hate me if I did?

It was so new, so foreign. And part of me wanted to be mad at Stefon for ruining the charade, but how could I be upset at him for owning who he was?

I drove across town to Halfway Café and parked next to Stefon's car. I could see him through the café's big windows, sitting at a table with two cups. He knew my coffee order so well I never even had to order for myself.

Taking a breath, I pushed through the doors and went to sit with him. My eyes raked him over, looking for signs of harm, for signs of pain. But he looked light. Free in a way that I'd never seen him be before, even that night he climbed through my window.

"Hey," he said, smiling at me. Even his smile looked easier.

"How are you?" I asked, hoping my assumptions were right.

"I'm great. My parents on the other hand..."

My stomach sank. "What did they say?"

"They didn't. Not really, anyway. We didn't speak at all on the ride home, and when we got inside, Mom said she was just crying because she wouldn't have grandbabies." He rolled his eyes. "As if I was thinking of babies at eighteen anyway."

"But then she calmed down?" I asked.

"Oh yeah. She got on her computer and started looking up facts about gay teens and how to parent them." He shook his head. "All she had to do was go on with her life."

I drank in the information, living vicariously

through him, worried about him. "What about your dad? Is he okay with it?"

"He said he was surprised, and that's it."

"So overall?" I asked.

"As good as I could have hoped." He took a sip of his caramel macchiato. "I wasn't expecting them to kick me out or anything, but I wasn't expecting them to throw a parade like Xiomara's parents either."

Xiomara's parents had gone all in, donating to the school to have anti-bullying speakers come talk about LGBT students, and her mom had organized the parade my parents wanted me to avoid.

I admired her in so many ways... not because she was good at volleyball, because, ouch. But she was cute with big brown eyes and a smile that touched every inch of her face, and because of how bravely she was herself. She hadn't stood in the cafeteria and announced herself as a lesbian like in some movie, but the rumors had spread, and she'd held her head high, not bothering to ignore or indulge them.

"Did you tell your parents when you got home?" Stefon asked, too much hope in his voice.

I shook my head. "I was too afraid. I can't believe you did it in front of everyone."

"I wasn't sure I'd actually go through with it," he admitted, looking out the window. The light caught his dark brown eyes, lightening them slightly. "I know your family's more conservative than mine, and I didn't want you to have to be the one to tell them about me."

I titled my head, realizing that he had considered me. "Thank you."

He smiled back at me, looking more... himself than ever before. Like a weight had been lifted off his shoulders. I wondered if I would ever feel that way. If I would ever be ready.

"What made you decide to come out?" I asked. "I mean, I know we talked about it. But talking about it and doing it... Those are two very different things."

He stirred his spoon around his mug. "I've been pretending for four years, longer than that, and the thought of pretending in college... I couldn't do it."

"I wish we could have forever," I admitted sadly.

"You heard your aunt ask about a pregnancy. They would have kept expecting us to go further. To get married, have babies." He shook his head. "I couldn't handle it anymore. And Dillon didn't want to have to sneak around with me. In fact..." Stefon grinned toward the door. "There he is."

I raised my eyebrows. "*What?!*" I spun toward the door, where a white guy was walking inside. He was wearing rolled jeans with stylish ankle boots and a gray shirt with a rainbow heart on the front.

"That's him," Stefon said, so much joy in his voice. "That's Dillon."

My mouth fell open into a surprised grin as I looked between the guy walking toward us and Stefon. This was Stefon's *boyfriend*. And if Stefon could have a boyfriend going into college... what was possible for me?

XIOMARA

DEE STOOD in the bathroom with me, helping to curl my hair for the parade. It was a beautiful day, not an ounce of wind, but plenty warm, so we opted for an updo with curls framing my face. Usually I just wore my hair straight down or in a ponytail, but it was nice to feel pretty sometimes.

She even did my makeup and said, "I actually have a surprise for you."

"What is it?" I asked as she went to her purse and pulled out a small package.

She held it up, showing a rainbow heart. "It's a temporary tattoo. I thought it would be cute to put it on our cheeks!"

"I love it!" I said. "Way better than the *rainbow*

chaps Mom and Dad are wearing to chaperone the prom."

Dee looked equal parts horrified and amused. "You're kidding. I know you're not, but you're kidding."

I shook my head. "She showed them to me last night."

"You have to love how she's gone all out for you since you came out," Dee said.

"That's just our mom, isn't it?" I said. "Remember when Luci liked that indie band so Mom put a cardboard cutout of the lead singer next to her seat at the table?"

We snorted with laugher, and Dee said, "She wrote him letters!"

"I almost forgot that! I can't believe he wrote back with that signed picture. Probably just so Mom would stop bothering him."

Dee chuckled. "And that time Dani decided she wanted to be a special effects makeup artist? I'm pretty sure Mom walked around with plastic pieces stuck to her face for a year."

I laughed. "The dragon look was pretty good."

"And I'm still trying to forget the petting zoo she had for my seventeenth birthday after I signed up to study animal science."

Now my belly was aching. "I think that was the first and last time the Emerson Police ever had to chase a potbelly pig down main street."

"That wasn't Mom's fault. Stupid Grant let it out."

"True," I said.

Dee grabbed a washcloth and wet it in the sink. "Now stop talking so I can put this on." She applied the tattoo to my cheek, careful not to get my skin too wet and ruin my makeup.

I stayed still, thinking about our parents. Mom was definitely the kind of person who went all out. She told me once that she wanted to be a mom from the time she was a child. Dad was the perfect match for her, low-key but fun enough to go along with all of her shenanigans.

Once Dee was done applying my tattoos, she applied her own, and I glanced at my phone. "I should get going. I don't want to be too late."

"Dad and I will be watching from the porch. Be sure to remember the little people."

I laughed and gave her a hug. "*Te amo,* sis."
"*Yo también.*"

Dad wished me luck as I left the house, and I was thankful for the walk down Main Street to collect myself. I could already see the houses decorated, the power lines done up with rainbow flags. People were beginning to mill about, setting out their chairs in preparation for the parade. It was kind of amazing that the Emerson Pride Association, with my mom's leadership, had brought this all together. That people were actually going to come.

I felt like royalty walking down the sidewalk in my overall shorts that had a rainbow heart on the front with Chucks and long rainbow socks. Even the bow in my updo was colorful and fun. I couldn't wait to see pictures from the day. Couldn't wait to see what everyone else would wear. From pictures of other parades online, it would be amazing.

After about a mile of walking, I reached the starting point of the parade. There were multiple floats lined up, and the community band was standing in formation with their instruments. Emerson Dance Studio had dancers in colorful uniforms. And at the head of it all was my mom.

She was speaking with someone on a float, offering directions, a bullhorn hanging in her hand. She looked both adorable and ridiculous in her big rainbow tulle tutu and a tight white tank that said PRIDE on the front.

I walked up to her and tapped her shoulder.

She turned and smiled at me, taking my face in

her hands. "You look beautiful! Do you see the Academy's float?"

"I just got here," I said. "Where is it?"

She pointed farther down the side street where everyone was lining up. "Fourth one back. Ollie's already there."

"Great," I said.

She gripped my fingers for a moment. "*Suerte.*" *Good luck.*

"Thanks, Mom," I said. I left her to her duties and walked back to the float. It was technically a pickup, decked top to bottom in a colorful version of the Academy logo and the Latin motto. *Ad Meliora.* Toward better things. I couldn't help but feel like this celebration of love and all different kinds of people was *better things*. And I was a part of it.

As I drew closer, I saw Ollie sitting on one of the throne chairs in the back, tapping on his phone.

"Hey," I called, approaching him. He looked cute. A rainbow headband held back his curly hair, and his white shirt said EMERSON LOVES GAY PEOPLE in big bright letters. "Nice shirt," I said with a giggle.

"I'm thinking about selling it," he joked.

"You'd make a fortune," I replied, looking

around for a way to get on the float. "How do I get up here?"

"Oh..." He walked to the back and found the tailgate lever under a bunch of colored paper. Once it was down, he extended his hand and helped me up.

"Thanks," I said, readjusting my socks and hair.

"No problem."

I followed him to the folding chairs meant for us. "Is Birdie excited to drive the float?"

He laughed. "That's an understatement."

"I can't wait to see her outfit."

She danced up to us, singing, "Did someone say outfit?"

My jaw dropped open. She was dressed in a rainbow suit and spinning a rainbow umbrella over her head. A rainbow top hat held down her curly blond hair.

"What do you think?" she asked, doing a spin.

"Epic," I replied. "I *have* to get a picture."

She posed with the umbrella, kicking her back heel up, and I snapped a picture. "Okay if I post it on social?"

"Of course."

I immediately uploaded it with the caption, *Best guidance counselor EVER.*

"Are you two ready?" she asked.

"All set," Ollie said.

"Same here."

"Good." She reached into the truck and pulled out a couple buckets of candy. "To throw for the kids. I thought it would be a nice touch."

"Only if I don't eat it all," I teased, making her and Ollie laugh.

My mom's voice came over the bullhorn and said, "WE'RE STARTING THE PARADE! FIRST FLOAT LEAVING... NOW!"

Cheering began around us, along with music from the community band. I couldn't help but smile, because all I felt in this moment was pure *joy*.

TWELVE

KIYANA

STEFON AND DILLON sat across from me, holding hands and sitting so close their shoulders touched. We were getting some looks, but not too many more than usual. And no one had said anything.

Not when Dillon told me about his work with the LGBTQ+ community at Elmbrooke University. Not when he said he'd been out since the age of twelve. Not even when he hugged Stefon tight and said how happy he was to be out in public with him or how proud he was of Stefon for coming out.

It was like living on a different planet, one where Stefon didn't have to work so hard to *hide*. And one where I was starting to wonder... why did I?

"Come with us to the parade," Stefon said, still holding hands with Dillon.

I blinked, coming out of my thoughts. "The parade?"

Dillon nodded. "The one on Main Street?"

"Right, right," I said. Of course I knew about it. I just hadn't planned to be anywhere near it. Guilt by association, right?

At my hesitation, Stefon said, "Just because you go to a parade doesn't automatically mean everyone will think you're gay." He knew me too well.

"Right," Dillon said. "I'm sure plenty of allies will be there too."

I felt nervous, like I always did before a big cheer competition, but excited too. Like I was about to do something so forbidden and off limits that would lead to a massive adventure. "I'll go," I said. "With you."

"Yes!" Stefon reached across the table and squeezed my hand. "I can already tell college is going to be amazing for us."

Dillon said, "College is the best. You're going to love it."

I sure hoped so. "I'll drive my car over there. Where should we meet?"

Stefon and Dillon glanced at each other, as

though they were already so in sync. I had to ask Stefon later why he hadn't told me about Dillon sooner. Surely he knew his secrets were safe with me.

"Maybe Main and Eighth?" Stefon said.

"I'll see you there." We all got up, and I lifted my purse strap over my shoulder. Dillon and Stefon got in Stef's car, and I got in mine, and I realized there was something else amongst my nerves.

I was feeling *lonely*. For the last four years, Stefon had been my person. I told him everything, even things I didn't say to my best girl friends on the cheerleading squad. But I had to be honest with myself.

Stefon wasn't my boyfriend. He was my friend. And there had been a part of me, deep down, that knew what we had couldn't last. Soon we'd be out in the "real world" teachers always talked about, living life on our own for the first time ever.

Stefon had already started living his.

Maybe it was time for me to do the same.

There was so many ways I knew how to exist as a lesbian—not make a face when someone made a joke about gay people or used the word "gay" as an insult. Keep my eyes down when my grandparents spoke about the "right" way to live. Ignore comments from my parents about me marrying Stefon someday and making babies with him.

But I had no idea how to flirt with girls, how to tell if they were gay or straight or even interested in me. Maybe that was part of it, figuring out how to exist as a gay person when the world defaulted to straight.

The road was getting busier and slower the closer I got to Main Street, and that exciting tingling was back. These people were here to celebrate who I was, not to tear it down. Just the thought brought a smile to my face. I wasn't alone, no matter how much I may have felt that way.

I parked along a side street and began walking toward the crossroads of Eighth and Main. It wasn't super crowded, but there was a good turnout. I looked amongst all the people and saw Dillon and Stefon walking toward me, holding hands.

I wondered what it felt like for them... to hold the hand of someone they liked.

Stefon and I had only ever held hands out of obligation, and I'd felt... safe, supported, but never those excited jitters I read about in books or heard people talk about on TV.

I looked up from their clasped hands and into their faces. "Do you know when it's starting?"

The sound of music played far away, and Stefon grinned. "Now?"

"Should we sit?" Dillon asked, gesturing at an open space on the sidewalk.

I nodded. "Let me run and grab a blanket from my car. I have one in the trunk."

"Want me to come with you?" Stefon offered.

I almost said yes. I was so used to having him by my side. But I shook my head and smiled. Things were different now. "Hang out with Dillon. I'll be right back."

I walked back toward my car, the sound of my flip-flops against the sidewalk keeping pace with the drumbeats far away. I could get used to being on my own, with enough practice. And what was possible for me now without my obligation to Stefon? A romance? An adventure?

I hoped so.

I pulled the blanket from my trunk, shook out what was left of sand from the beach, and walked back toward Main Street. From here, I could see a craftsman house across the way, completely decked out with pride decorations. From the windows to the flags along the front entrance, everything was done to the hilt.

I wondered who lived in that house. If they were a gay couple themselves, if they had a child who was trans maybe. The thought of there being so much support there made me smile.

When I reached Stefon and Dillon, Stef took the blanket and spread it on the sidewalk for us. Stefon sat in between the two of us, and I couldn't help but think this was the perfect picture, the poetic transition between his old life and his new one.

I held up my phone and said, "We have to take a selfie."

We all grinned at the camera, and I froze the moment forever, wanting to remember that if Stefon could do this, so could I.

"Oh, look!" Dillon said, pointing down the street.

I followed his finger to see the start of the parade turning the corner. The first vehicle was the sheriff's pickup, with something rainbow on the top. As they drew closer, I realized it was EPD in colorful letters.

Behind the sheriff was a group of dancers in beautiful costumes, spinning and twirling. Up close,

I recognized one of the younger girls from the cheer squad dancing. She hadn't even mentioned it, but it made me happy.

"GO, LIVVY!" I yelled, and Stefon yelled, "GO, LIV!"

She looked at us for a moment, then did a doubletake, her mouth falling wide open. She clearly hadn't expected to see us here, but what other conclusions she had drawn in that split second, I didn't know. Maybe it had been a bad idea to cheer for her. To make her look our way.

But then again, Stefon had cheered too.

Following the dancers were a few floats from local businesses. Seaton Bakery. Waldo's Diner. Vestido. I couldn't believe all of them had gone to so much effort to support the cause.

Then my mouth fell open. Emerson Academy had put a whole float together? Then I saw who was sitting on the back. Ollie Bardot, who had graduated several years before me and staged a massive coup to keep Birdie working there. And then... Xiomara.

She looked cute in her overalls with her hair all curly and done up. There was a rainbow heart tattooed on her cheek, just like the cheerleaders always wore fake tattoos of feather quills to football games.

But her eyes were stuck on something behind me, higher up.

I turned to see what she was looking at, and my heart constricted. The apartment windows above had been painted with anti-gay phrases. It was the same sorts of things I'd heard before, but now, at the parade, it felt so wrong. This wasn't a day to tear people down… It was a day to celebrate.

And I wanted to celebrate a smile on Xiomara's face instead of the hurt look she wore now.

"Go, Xiomara! Ow owww!" I yelled, grinning all the while.

She rewarded me by looking away from the windows and looking at me, a surprised smile on her face. It was adorable. Beautiful. Like the summer sun shining on my skin. She reached into a bucket and threw some candy my way.

I caught it, thinking this moment couldn't get any sweeter.

Then Stefon yelled beside me, "Go, Xi!" And so did Dillon. "Go, Xi!"

And then soon, everyone around us was chanting, "Go, Xi! Go, Xi! Go, Xi!" as her float slowly drove by.

THIRTEEN

WHAT HAD JUST HAPPENED?

I could still hear the echoes of the crowd chanting my name as the float continued toward the end of Main Street.

Ollie leaned over, grinning, and said, "If I didn't know any better, I'd say you have a secret admirer."

I raised my eyebrows. "Who?"

"That girl who yelled your name. I saw the way she smiled at you."

"She's a cheerleader," I said. "Or was—she just graduated. And I hit her in the head with a volley-ball last week."

"And cheerleaders can't be gay?" he asked.

I laughed. "No, she's just good at... cheering," I

finished lamely, my mind already going over every single moment of what happened.

I'd been distracted, heartbroken by the messages I'd seen painted on the apartments across from my house, and then I'd heard someone cheering for me. Even louder than my dad and Dee had been from across the street on our front porch steps.

When I looked, I'd seen two of the most popular people at my school, Stefon and Kiyana, along with a guy I didn't recognize. But Stefon had been holding that guy's hand. And Kiyana had been smiling at me...

Wait. Was Stefon gay?

Had Kiyana known?

I had so many questions swirling through my mind as Ollie said, "Kids at three o'clock."

I glanced around—because really, who memorized directions based on a clock face—and found a group of kids dancing in front of their parents sitting in folding chairs. They had their hands in the air, hoping for candy from us, and I grinned, passing them some.

They dove for the candy bars and suckers, and I smiled at their joy. They looked so happy. So carefree. I had probably looked like that at some point.

I wondered when life had changed for me.

From that happy abandon to the should and shouldn'ts of life. Probably somewhere at the beginning of elementary school, when everyone around me had "boyfriends" and "girlfriends" and I was more interested in my comic books than a relationship.

My parents had never been homophobic. Never said a bad word about gay people—but when "faggot" was thrown around on the playground as an insult and people called things they didn't like "gay"... I think something told me deep down that my preferences were something to be ashamed of. Something to be hidden.

And if this parade had done anything, it had shown me that this joy, this love, it didn't belong in the background of any story. It deserved to be up front and center.

We reached the end of Main Street, and the floats sped up slightly, getting us back to the starting point, where they could be dismantled and driven away.

Ollie helped me off the back, holding my hand as I jumped down, and he gave me a high five. "How did it feel? Being up there for everyone to see?"

"Not as bad as I thought it might," I admitted,

thinking of Kiyana's smile all the while. "Are you going to the festival?"

He nodded. "I'm actually hosting a booth to sell all my propagations from my ivies and succulents."

"Nice," I said. "I guess I'll see you there?"

"It's a plan."

Birdie came to us and hugged Ollie. Then she gave me a one-armed hug. "You did so wonderful, Xi!"

"Thank you," I said, smiling because her energy was just so contagious. "Great driving, by the way. Very straight."

She laughed. "I guess it was bad for this parade then."

I giggled too, and Mom approached, saying, "What's so funny?"

"You had to be there," Birdie said with a grin.

Mom gave me a hug and said, "I need to go make sure the booths get set up for the festival, but I wanted to tell you how fabulous you were! And everyone chanting your name?" She wiped at tears pooling in her eyes. "I'm *so* proud of you."

I hugged her back. "It wouldn't have happened without you," I said. It was the truth. Mom had given me so much today, in so many ways.

She fanned her eyes. "I'm going to cry."

Saving the day, Birdie took my mom's hand and said, "How can I help with the festival?"

They began making plans, and I excused myself, saying I was going to grab a snack at the house before going to the festival.

The street had mostly emptied, save the few people mingling and talking amongst themselves. But as I got closer to my house, I saw people I recognized on the sidewalk.

Kiyana, Stefon, and mystery guy...

I was about to cross the street to give them a wide berth, feeling old embarrassment from the volleyball fiasco, but Stefon waved me over.

I nearly had to look behind me because Stefon and I had never talked. I mean, never.

He was a popular football player, a senior, and way too cool to be seen anywhere near me. And cheerleaders were usually oil to my water, as proven at the pool... What did they want to talk to me about?

As I got closer, I reminded myself that they had come to the pride parade. They had cheered for me. And they were nice enough that Ollie thought Kiyana might have had a crush on me. It would be okay. As long as I didn't trip over an invisible line and embarrass myself.

"Hey, Xi," Kiyana said.

I liked the way she said my nickname. Her voice was low and smooth, and the familiarity of the nickname... I liked it.

Maybe I wasn't so oil-water with cheerleaders after all.

"Hi," I said, trying to channel my most confident version of myself. "I didn't know you were coming to the parade."

Stefon smiled at the guy holding his hand, "My boyfriend, Dillon, and I convinced Ki to come."

Clearly it was a new relationship because Dillon looked very pleased, and I'd seen Stefon and Kiyana together at graduation just a couple weeks ago. I wanted to ask more, but I didn't want to be rude.

"Did you have fun?" I asked Kiyana.

She didn't quite meet my eyes at first, but when she did, it was like the sun coming over the horizon. All bright and consuming. "I had a great time. You were really good up there."

"Thanks," I said, smiling more easily now. "Are you all going to the festival?"

"Actually," Stefon said, "Dillon and I need to pick something up from his car before we go. Maybe you two can ride together?"

Kiyana gave him a look I didn't quite understand, then turned back to me with a warm smile. "That would be fun... if you want to."

Had I just entered some sort of alternate universe? Was this a prank? Both seemed more likely than me spending time at a pride festival with a hot cheerleader who I'd recently injured with a rogue volleyball.

Despite all my fears, I leaned into my excitement and said, "Okay."

FOURTEEN

KIYANA

AS MY EX-FAKE-BOYFRIEND and his new *real* boyfriend took off the other way, Xiomara and I stood awkwardly on the sidewalk. I'd never had troubles talking to people before, but standing across from her... I felt tongue-tied.

"I'm sorry," she said quickly.

I raised my eyebrows. "Why?" What did she have to be sorry for?

"For the volleyball thing." She still wouldn't meet my eyes, instead looking down at the side-walk, her long dark lashes fanning over her cheeks.

I bit my lip. "I already forgot about it." More like I was distracted by how cute you are.

Her smile hit me again, just as warm as before.

"Do you mind if I grab my purse from my house before we go?" she asked.

I nodded, eager to see any insight into her life. It may have sounded silly, but I was desperate to know what it was like for her to live as a lesbian. What did her room look like? Was it... normal?

"It's right over there." She jerked her thumb over her shoulder at the overly decorated house.

"Your house is adorable," I said, following her across the now quiet street. Why hadn't I guessed that it could be hers? If anyone would do their house up like that, it would be Xiomara's parents. They'd been so involved at our school, making sure it was an inclusive environment for their daughter.

But high schoolers were crappy sometimes, and no number of flyers or inspirational speakers could change that. One of the main reasons I'd stayed silent.

We reached the front steps, where someone had written in chalk LOVE IS LOVE, and I smiled at the steps. "Is it okay if I come inside?"

She looked me over like she was worried I might not like what I saw. I already knew that was impossible.

But then the front door opened, and a man who I instantly recognized as Xiomara's father said,

"Hey, Xi. Oh, I didn't realize you were out here with someone..." He looked confused. "Kiyana, right? You're a cheerleader, yeah?" The curious way he took me in made me feel completely exposed.

I nodded, my cheeks already feeling hot. Maybe Xi was right to expect me to run. Just being with her was like being lesbian by association. And I hated that I felt that way. Just because I hung out with Xi and was a girl didn't instantly mean I was dating her. This internalized homophobia was hard to get over.

Her dad smiled warmly at me and said, "Dee and I just made some *polvorones*. Want to taste-test them for us?"

Xi smiled at me. "They're so good. You should try some."

"Okay," I said, putting a practiced smile on my face and following them inside.

Their home was just as bright and cheery on the inside as the décor was on the outside. There were big photos of Xi and her sisters, pieces of bright art on the walls, and blooms of flowers on almost every table. It didn't feel carefully curated and sterile like my home so often did. It felt like everything was meant to be here.

For the first time since last night, I felt my whole

body exhale. My shoulders loosen. Everything about this place said *home*.

We walked through their living room and into a kitchen with a blue and orange tiled backsplash. Dee stood by the stove with a spatula, taking little colorful cookies off of wax paper. The sugary smell was just as heavenly as the rest of the house.

"They look great," I said.

Dee turned and gave me a surprised look. "Kiyana?"

"Hey," I said. "Long time no see." We hardly ever saw each other in high school, to be honest, even though she was only a year older than me. We ran in different circles that only rubbed shoulders occasionally—her with the softball team and me with the cheerleaders and football players.

"How's Stefon?" Dee asked.

"He's doing great. He actually just came out," I said, wanting to talk to someone about it who would understand.

Xi didn't look as surprised like her dad and sister, but Dee had a big grin on her face.

"Good for him! How are you taking it?"

I glanced at Xi. Part of me wanted to admit that I was a lesbian, right then and there. That I'd like nothing more than to take Xi's hand and weave my fingers through hers. But something held me back. "If I'm being honest, I've known for a while."

"Wow." Xi's dad said. "How are his parents taking it? Can you let him know if he needs anything at all, we're here for him?"

I nodded. "I think they're going to be okay, but I'll definitely let him know."

"Great," he replied, a kind smile in his eyes. They looked so much like Xi's. Or Xi's looked like his. Whichever. They were beautiful.

He reached into a cabinet and pulled out a few small plates, handing them to Dee. "I asked Kiyana and Xiomara to check our work."

Dee laughed, the sound contagious. "I think we've tested enough. But I'm happy to share." She winked at me.

They handed me a plate of the little cookies first, and I picked one up, the dough still warm under my fingertips. I took a careful bite of the chocolate portion, and the sweet crumbles had the best flavor. "So good," I said before I even finished chewing.

Xi's dad smirked. "That's because Xi didn't help."

"Hey!" Xi cried. "It's not my fault I didn't get the baking gene. You only have yourself to blame."

He chuckled, taking a bite of his own cookie. "Three out of four isn't bad."

Shaking her head, Xi said, "I'm going to grab my purse. Don't say anything crazy while I'm gone." She gave me a quick smile that narrowed the corners of her almond eyes and hurried toward the stairs.

Alone with her dad and sister, I took another bite of the cookie, loving the crumbly texture and sweet flavors. Even though the colors were bright, the flavors were more subtle.

"Any plans for college in the fall?" her dad asked, making conversation. But not in the way that most people did—like they were just trying to fill the quiet. He seemed actually interested.

"I'm going to Elmbrooke, just an hour and a half from here."

"Ah, they have a great finance program. We get interns from there from time to time."

A sense of relief swept over me that he recognized the college. Everyone had wanted me to go to an Ivy League school like Stanford, but our guidance counselor had encouraged me to follow my heart and pursue cheerleading instead. She said if I wanted to be a collegiate cheer coach someday, it would be good to have the experience.

"What are you studying?" Dee asked.

"Business," I replied. It was general enough to give me lots of options, which I definitely needed if cheer coaching didn't work out right away.

"Nice," Xi's dad said. "Are you planning to go to the prom later today?"

"The prom?" I asked. "It was a couple weeks back."

His smile crinkled his eyes. "The inclusive prom tonight. Xi and her friends actually helped decorate the whole thing. There's going to be a professional DJ and everything."

From behind me, Xi said, "She doesn't have to go if she doesn't want to. Especially considering what you're wearing."

I raised my eyebrows toward her dad. "What are you wearing?"

Her dad's cheeks reddened slightly, and he mumbled something about it being Mrs. Muñoz's idea.

Xi reached into a cabinet, taking out a plastic bag, and filled it with *polvorones* "for the road" and then we left the house, her dad and sister waving behind us.

"I hope they didn't say anything too embarrass-ing," Xi said as we made our way toward her car.

"Not at all." Out of the corner of my eye, I spotted the signs she'd focused on earlier, and they were such a contrast to the bright and cheery place we'd come from.

Following my gaze, Xi said, "I wasn't expecting to see that. It sucks knowing that they look at my house every day and see something they hate."

I shook my head, appalled that anyone could hate the Muñoz family. "It's their problem, not yours." And for the first time... I believed it.

I'd spent all of high school worrying what people would think of me if they knew who I really was. In reality, if they didn't like me, they were missing out. Regardless of my sexual orientation, I was fun to be around, dedicated to the things that mattered to me, and loyal as could be. Anyone who wanted to focus on one part of me and hate the whole of who I was had to be missing out.

And maybe I had been missing out too, by not allowing people to love all of who I was. So, I glanced over to Xiomara, the light glancing off her brown hair almost giving it a reddish hue, and said, "Tell me about this prom."

FIFTEEN

XIOMARA

THE WAY her amber eyes studied me with a soft smile playing along her lips left me breathless. I was thankful for the distraction of her car so I could open the door and gather myself before telling her about the prom that I'd be attending dateless.

Unless there was a possibility...

No. I needed to stop hoping for things that could never happen in a million years.

I sat in her car, surrounded by the sweet smell of her perfume, and began speaking about the event. "It's an inclusive prom, and the theme is 'Under the Sea.' It's a cliché, but on purpose."

"What do you mean?" she asked.

"For a lot of people who have RSVP'd, this will be

their first prom ever. They missed out on their prom in high school because they were afraid of being judged, or in some cases, they weren't even allowed to go."

Kiyana smiled. "I'm so glad they can go now." But her smile quickly faltered. I couldn't tell what she was thinking, and quite frankly, I was afraid to ask. It was like our time together was one of Abuela's crochet projects, and pulling a single thread could have the entire thing unraveling.

"Thank you," I said, fidgeting with the mood ring around my thumb.

"Can I ask you something?" Kiyana said.

I braced myself and said, "Okay."

"What did you think when you saw Stefon and his boyfriend?"

That was the last question I expected. In fact, I never knew people like her or Stefon even cared about the thoughts of unpopular underclassmen like me. But here she was, stopped at a red light and glancing my way for an answer.

"I mean... it was cool to see them at the parade together," I finally said.

"But were you surprised? Did you expect him to like guys?"

"After dating you for four years? Not at all." I

cringed slightly. "For me, the thought of dating a guy for a week, much less a year, is... not good."

I felt like I was fumbling over my words, not stringing them together in a way that made me seem interesting or even fun, but Kiyana seemed satisfied.

"Did you suspect it before he told you?" I asked, tugging gently on one of those metaphorical strands.

Kiyana only shook her head.

Interesting.

"How did you feel about it when you found out?" I asked, holding my breath as I waited for her answer. "Are you sad that he's not your boyfriend anymore?"

Kiyana shrugged, keeping her eyes on the road as she drove through town, closer to Emerson Trails, where the festival was being held. "I'm happy for him." She glanced toward me, and one look in her eyes told me she was sincere. "But I am sad that our relationship won't be the same."

"I get that. When Van got a girlfriend, things were different. She was always around, and I feel like she thought Shelly and I were a threat to their relationship."

"Did she get over it?" Kiyana asked. "The girlfriend?"

"After a while, it was like she'd been one of our best friends all along." I wondered if it would feel that way with Gunnar and Shelley if they stayed together. The thought of being the only one in my group without a partner felt heavy on my chest. I would be the only one flying solo.

"Are your friends going to be at the festival?" she asked.

I nodded. We'd been planning to meet there. And I couldn't imagine how stunned they'd be to see Kiyana with me.

I sent them a quick text with a heads-up and then put my phone back in my purse. But the silence was deafening. After all, what did Kiyana and I really have in common? I was a soon-to-be junior harboring a secret crush, and she was a straight high school graduate leaving for college shortly.

She slowed the car, and I looked out the window, realizing we were almost there. Maybe it was better we went our separate ways now. Before people saw us together and made assumptions that couldn't be further from the truth.

As soon as the car stopped, I said, "Thanks for

the ride. I can get out first, and if you wait a few minutes, I don't think anyone will notice we came together."

A tiny little crease formed between her eyebrows. "Why would I want to do that?"

"Well, people's minds like to jump to conclusions, and if they saw me alone with you, they might think..." Suddenly, the air in the car felt very thick, and my throat constricted on the words. *They might think we're together.*

"They might think what?" Kiyana said, holding my gaze.

"That we're... That you're... with me." I felt self-conscious. Like she was seeing too much. Of what, I wasn't exactly sure. Did she catch my doubled chin? My carefully tweezed eyebrows or the heart on my cheek? What about the dark brown of my eyes or the way my baby hairs always stuck out despite using massive amounts of hairspray? And more importantly, what did she think when she saw those things?

She smiled slightly, her full lips quirking up at the corner. They were beautiful, transitioning from ebony to pink in the most stunning way, like God himself had painted them with the shades he loved the most. "What would be so wrong with us being together?" she asked, her lips moving around the words, giving hints of her straight, white teeth.

My gut ached at the unfulfilled wish. I wanted to have a girlfriend to hold my hand, to kiss my lips, to tuck my hair behind my ear like they always did so romantically in the movies. And yeah, it would be even better if that girl was as beautiful as Kiyana. But my life was not a fantasy. Of that, I was certain.

Kiyana glanced around like someone might hear or see us through the protection of her car in the parking lot, then faced me again. "Can you keep a secret?"

I only nodded. It was all I *could* do. The air was so charged between us, it felt like I was standing at the edge of a cliff, unsure of whether I would fall or fly.

She bit her lip, making my insides squirm. "Stefon and I... we came up with a deal our freshman year. We would date each other and keep everyone from knowing the truth."

"And what was the truth?" I breathed.

She reached out and touched my hand, ran her fingertips along my skin, making goosebumps rise on my arms. "That he likes guys. And I...like girls."

The butterflies in my stomach were dancing

now, realizing just how close I was to Kiyana. Dangerously aware of her hand still on mine. I couldn't believe what she was saying, what I was *feeling*.

She looked from my hand to my eyes. "What do you think about that?" she asked, her chest just as still as mine.

Dodging the question altogether for fear of giving myself away too early, I asked, "Who else knows?"

"Only Stefon and now you."

SIXTEEN

KIYANA

IT WAS like I was outside my body, watching this person move my lips. Move my hand.

Because the old Kiyana wouldn't be alone in a car with the only lesbian at school.

Old Kiyana wouldn't be reaching across the console and savoring the feeling of Xi's soft skin under her fingertips.

Old Kiyana would never reveal her deepest secret.

And old Kiyana wouldn't be waiting with bated breath, caring more than anything about what Xiomara would say.

But then Xi cracked one of those smiles that was like the dawn—inevitable, transformative, and she whispered, "I don't want to admit how happy that makes me."

Her response brought a smile to my own lips. "It feels good to be myself, even if it's only with you."

Xiomara squeezed my hand in return, and it was... *everything*. Nothing like the comforting, brotherly feel of holding Stefon's hand. The contact jerked me right back into my own body, and I was feeling it *all*. My heart raced, my skin tingled, and every nerve ending was on red alert for what could possibly come next.

"Should we go check out the festival?" she asked.

I looked down at our hands, terrified of losing what I was feeling in this moment. "Honestly?"

"Yeah?"

"I'd rather be somewhere with you." If we were at the festival, there would be so much pressure. So much worry about how people saw us. I wanted to explore this with her, without the wandering and assuming eyes of others.

The flush on her cheeks was just as cute as her smile. "I have an idea where we can go."

"Yeah?"

Her stomach growled in response, and I

laughed, all the tension releasing from my chest like a stream of tiny bubbles.

"Let's get some food first."

She put in a to-go order at Waldo's Diner, saying she had been planning on festival food for lunch, and I got a milkshake and fries to have with her. But after that, our destination was a mystery.

When we arrived at the restaurant, she went inside to pick up the order, declining my offer to help pay. Without her, my car felt so much emptier than before. Being around Xi was natural, in a way completely different to hanging out with Stefon. I liked the way little strands of hair fell around her face—liked the way she snuck glances at me when she thought I wasn't watching.

As she walked out the door, the sun caught her eyes, her hair, and she smiled at me through my windshield. Why had I never noticed how special her smiles were? Had I really never looked her way, or had I kept myself from doing so for fear of what I'd find? What I'd feel?

She opened the door and got in, passing me a Styrofoam cup. "Chocolate, as promised."

"Thank you," I said, taking a drink. It was so good. "Now we just need some plovornes to go with it."

Xi giggled.

"What?" I asked.

"It's *polvorones*," she said, slowing down each syllable. Watching her full lips form the word was far too distracting. "Try it."

"Pol—" I tried.

"Vo," she encouraged.

I copied after her until she wore a satisfied smile. "Not quite native, but I'll take it," she said.

I laughed. "I knew I should have chosen Spanish instead of French."

"Spanish would be much less useful in Paris. Your family went there after graduation, right?"

How did she know that? Had she been paying attention to me all this time? The thought was...flattering.

At my silence, she said, "I thought I saw something on social media."

"It was beautiful there, but not like I always dreamed it would be."

"What do you mean?" she asked, seeming genuinely interested in my thoughts on the place, not just in what I'd brought home or if I'd met any Frenchmen, like my cheerleading friends had wanted to know. But then again, that made sense. I made sure my squad mates didn't know the deepest parts of me. Only the parts I thought they would like.

I thought back to Paris, the morning I had walked the city streets on my own while my parents ate at a café. "Everyone calls Paris the most romantic city in the world, but a lot of it was so loud and crowded. And it was more modern than I expected it to be. But there were beautiful parts too. There's this massive garden that surrounds the Eiffel Tower, and people brought blankets and little bottles of wine, just passing the time."

"It sounds amazing." There were stars in her eyes.

"Maybe you'll go someday," I said. And part of me wished I could be there to see the Eiffel Tower lights reflected in her eyes.

As I drove, she told me to take another turn, and I drew my eyebrows together. "We're going to the Academy?"

She grinned as I turned into the empty parking lot. "I wasn't sure if you were coming to the prom tonight, but I wanted you to see the decorations."

"I'd like that," I said. All the Emerson Academy proms were hosted at fancy hotels in grand ball-rooms. Never in the school gymnasium like at some public schools.

I was eager to see what they'd done with this place.

We got out of the car and walked through the empty parking lot of our school. Well, really, it was her school now.

I had so many memories of this place—of hanging out by Stefon's car before school with other cheerleaders and football players. I remembered the bench where I'd sat next to Stefon as he asked me to prom. The stairs were steep as ever, unforgiving after a hard practice with lots of leg work.

And then there was the inscription above the entrance—*Ad Meliora*. It meant toward better things, and if I was being honest, I didn't really think that was true for me. High school was supposedly the best years of your life, and it certainly looked that way on the outside. I had a handsome "boyfriend," had the plastic homecoming crown on display in my room, and spent more weekends at parties than alone at home. But underneath all the smiles and selfies, it had been there. The feeling like I didn't quite fit in. Like my whole life could come crashing down at any moment.

As I walked beside this girl who had bravely, publicly, been herself for the last year, I wondered if maybe she was the one who had it figured out all along.

She stopped outside the double doors to the gym and gave me one of those breathtaking smiles. "Are you ready for the gayest prom decorations ever?"

A giggle spilled out my lips. "Absolutely."

She pushed the door open and held it for me with her arm extended, Vanna White style. I felt the warmth of her body as I brushed past her and took it in. The space was incredible, with blue vinyl protecting the hardwood floors and all shades of blue tulle drawing down from a circular spot in the ceiling. There was a massive boat I thought I recognized from the last school play and tables topped with aquariums of fish.

Following my gaze, Xi said, "The fish are fake. But they look real from here, huh?"

"They do. It's beautiful, Xi," I said, turning to face her.

"Thank you." She smiled back at me. In the dim lighting, her olive skin was tinted blue, and I felt like a fish swimming in the deep, dark pools of her eyes.

It was so quiet here, just the two of us, and I

found myself wanting to kiss her. To taste her lips and feel her touch.

But my phone began ringing.

Xi looked away from me, touching a ring on her thumb, and I reached for my phone, seeing Stefon's name on the screen.

"Hello?" I said.

"Where are you?" he asked over the background noise. "They have a *bouncy slide.*"

"I..." I glanced toward Xi. I wasn't ready to share her. Not yet.

She gave me a questioning look, and I muted my speaker.

"Can it be my turn to show you something?" I asked.

She smiled, nodded.

"You don't mind missing the festival?"

She shook her head.

Relieved, I unmuted my phone and said to Stefon, "Have fun with Dillon. I'll call you later."

SEVENTEEN

XIOMARA

MY HEART MUST HAVE BEEN BEATING a million times a minute. For a moment there, I had thought... I had thought Kiyana wanted to kiss me. Her glittering brown eyes had flicked to my lips, and then she'd met my gaze again. Just the look had been electrifying. I couldn't imagine how her touch would feel.

But then Stefon had called, and I was still breathless.

She slipped her fingers through mine, leading me away from the gym and back to the parking lot. As soon as we exited the doors, she let her fingers fall from mine, and I tried not to be disappointed by the absence.

We got into her car, which smelled like her

perfume and the takeout from earlier. Intoxicating. "Where to now?" I asked.

Wearing a wicked smile, she said, "It's a surprise."

I laughed. "Or is it payback?"

"Maybe both," she replied with a wink.

I looked out the windows as she drove toward our unknown destination. "Can I ask you something—other than where we're going?"

"Sure."

"When are you planning on telling your parents?" I asked. I bit my lip, knowing this could very well be the question that ended it all, but I had to know. For me, hiding myself had been like living underneath a weighted blanket. At first it was comforting, but over time, it felt suffocating. Every word felt strained, every action measured. How she had managed such an act for so long... I could only imagine how exhausted she must have been.

She let out a humorless laugh. "Never? I don't know how they'd take it, but my grandparents would disown me."

A deep ache formed in my chest. I knew Abuela didn't understand me, but at least she loved me. "That's awful."

She nodded. "But so is the alternative." Her smile faltered, and then she said, "There it is."

I raised my eyebrows as we approached Emerson Tumbling, a gymnastic gym that I'd only set foot in once at six years old, and that had been more than enough. "What are we doing here?"

"You showed me something you created. I thought I'd show you mine."

Intrigued, I got out of her parked car and followed her through the empty parking lot toward the metal building. "Are we allowed to be here?"

She jangled her key ring. "It's not breaking and entering if you have a key."

That reminded me of something Lucy would say. As the second oldest, she had always broken more rules than she followed. Most of our parents' gray hairs could definitely be attributed to her.

Kiyana slipped the key into the lock and turned it, letting us into the big, open space filled with mats and hanging bars and more things I had no idea how to name, much less describe. The whole place smelled faintly of sweat and disinfectant.

"This is where we practice most of our stunts for cheerleading," Kiyana said, stepping farther inside. "But we just added a foam pit for the younger kids and an inflatable diving board."

"That sounds more my speed," I said. "The foam pit. Not the diving board. I'm pretty sure I'm the least coordinated person to ever set foot in here."

"Really?"

I nodded. "My mom signed me up for gymnastic lessons when I was six, and I somehow managed to kick the instructor in the face while doing a somersault, and then I knocked all the other girls over like dominoes while we were stretching."

"Stretching?" Kiyana said, giggling.

I gestured at my arms. "Weapons of mass destruction."

She rewarded me with a full laugh that shook her stomach and squinted her eyes. It was beautiful, the way she laughed. At the edge of the mat, she kicked off her flip-flops, and I bent to untie my Chucks. With only my rainbow socks left, I followed her across the mat to a corner of the gym.

The diving board was more like a launch pad over the foam pit. She climbed the steps, and at the top, cast a smile toward me over her shoulder before jumping in. She landed amongst the foam squares, bouncing in the pit before stilling.

"Join me!" she said, laughing.

"I can join you from here," I said at the edge of the pit.

"Chicken."

"As if peer pressure could work on me," I retorted.

"And puppy dog eyes?" She widened her eyes and stuck out her bottom lip in the most adorable way.

"Okay, maybe that's working," I said with a laugh. "You promise I won't get hurt?"

"The foam's four feet deep, and you'd have to be trying to miss the pit."

"It's as if you don't know me at all," I replied, moving toward the platform. I could do this, right? After all, I'd done tons of new things today. I'd ridden on the back of a float for the entire town to see. I was spending time with a cheerleader. And now she was asking me to jump.

Why the heck not?

Oh yeah, because it was high up here. I stood at the edge of the wobbly inflatable, staring down at Kiyana lounging amongst the foam squares, looking completely at peace. The exact opposite of the terror I felt in every inch of my body.

"Come on!" she called. "The water's warm!" She tossed a foam square at me, and in my attempt to dodge it, I lost my balance, toppling off the ledge and screaming all the way down to the pit. I landed face first with my mouth open on a foam square.

Kiyana's tinkling laugh was the first thing I heard after the blood stopped rushing through my ears and I realized I had not, in fact, succumbed to death by foam pit.

"That was awful!" I said, extracting at least my face from the squares. "Why did you make it look so fun?"

"Probably because it is." She was laughing, crawling toward me across the foam blocks, looking undoubtedly more graceful than me.

I pretended to pout, looking away from her. "My pride is wounded."

"You were adorable," she replied, close enough now for me to feel her movement shift the foam underneath me.

So maybe I didn't mind being called adorable.

I glanced her way just in time to see she was inches from me. So close. Despite the quiet in the gym, my mind was loud. Screaming that Kiyana was so near.

Close enough to kiss.

I looked into her eyes, wondering what was happening. Why she was interested. What had changed. But most of all, wondering what it would feel like to have her lips on mine.

I'd only dreamed of my first kiss, thought it was something months or even years away. But here she was. I could smell her minty gum on her breath. Could see the hole from an abandoned piercing on the right side of her nose.

I reached out and tapped the spot. "What happened?"

She took my hand in hers, holding it, looking at my fingers. Mine were large, bigger than most of the girls in my class, but Kiyana was a big girl too. Our hands matched, all except color. "I got my nose pierced on spring break with a friend one year. When my mom found out, she lost her mind. Made me take it out, threw away the piercing, called my friend's mom and chewed her out for letting me get a piercing in the first place."

I covered my mouth with my hand. "That must have been so embarrassing."

Kiyana rolled her eyes. "You have no idea. I was sitting at the end of the lunch table for a month after that."

"But you made your way back to the middle."

"Mostly because of Stefon."

I took her in, picturing a little stud shining in her nose. "You'd look cute with a nose ring."

Instead of replying, she studied me. "You look cute regardless."

My cheeks warmed with the rest of my insides, butterfly wings tickling my stomach. I may have been safely in the foam pit, but I felt like I was about to jump all over again.

My eyes drifted from hers to her lips, getting even closer.

And then my lids slid close and I felt her lips press to mine. Pure magic. Pure bliss.

EIGHTEEN

KIYANA

STEFON and I had kissed once, just to try it to see if we could convince ourselves to be something other than what we were, but it was *nothing* like this.

Kissing Xi was like breathing for the first time in my life. Exhilarating, exciting, and painful to know all I had been missing for oh-so long. She was soft against me, her lips like feathery pillows against mine. When I put my hand to the back of her neck, her skin was just as soft. And her body, pressing to mine now in the foam pit, had my heart racing, my breath speeding.

It was both the scariest and most natural thing I had ever done.

Her delicate tongue slid against my lips, and somewhere in my body, I knew to open my mouth, to let her in, to taste all she had to offer while savoring every second. She let out the sweetest moan against my lips, and it made butterflies flutter madly in my stomach.

Her fingers worked through the kinky hair at the base of my neck, and I moved my hand to her chest, feeling her heart race against my palm.

I smiled against her kiss, because I wasn't alone. She was feeling exactly as I did. All adrenaline and excitement pumping through my veins at record pace.

She kissed me deeper, not in a hurry to end our embrace, and neither was I.

We kissed. For minutes, hours, exploring sensations new to us both, letting our touches light our bodies on fire in flames we'd never experienced.

And when we finally pulled apart, our chests heaved with gasps of air because everything was different now.

I knew that I had to come out. I knew that I couldn't forgo this for the rest of my life.

I knew that I wanted to kiss, and be kissed, hold and be held, for the rest of my life.

Xi's eyes were wide, stunned, and she took me in. "That was..."

"Incredible," I finished, biting my tender bottom lip.

She giggled in the most adorable way, burying her face in the foam.

I reached out and took her hand, slipping my fingers through hers. I loved the way our skin contrasted. The way our fingers fit together, not one bigger or smaller than the other.

"I know this is crazy," she said, "but will you go to prom with me? I don't have a date yet, and it would be so fun to dance with you."

My heart stalled twice. Once at the thought of dancing with Xi. How beautiful she might look in a prom dress amidst a sea of twinkling lights. But then my heart stalled again at the thought of other people seeing us dancing together...

Word would spread so fast and get to my parents' ears before I was ready for them to know.

My hesitation had Xi looking down, looking away. "You don't want to," she said, her voice growing distant. "It's okay."

"I... can't," I finished.

She looked back to me, confused. "Why not? Are you busy?"

I couldn't lie. "I'm still not ready for anyone to know."

"I thought when you told me, it was because you were ready to come out..." Her lips pressed together as she tried to make the hurt on her face. "You don't want to be seen with me. I get it. I'm just another secret to you."

"Xi..."

"I know it's hard for you, I do." Her lips were trembling. "But do you know what it's like to be the only lesbian at school? The comments people make about me? You have no idea because you get to lead your perfect life as the popular cheerleader."

"You didn't have to come out," I replied. "No one was forcing you. But you're trying to force me before I'm ready, and that's not okay."

She studied me for a moment. "You're right. But I don't want to be someone's secret." She pushed herself on the foam, struggling to move to the edge. It was awkward and embarrassing, and I wished for the both of us we could be anywhere but here.

Just moments ago, I'd been so happy, but now I felt lower than ever, guilty for the way I'd used Xi. Maybe she was right—I'd wanted to know what it was like to kiss a girl, but I hadn't thought of what would happen after.

It wasn't fair to her to be kept in the shadows. If

the parade had shown anything, she belonged in the spotlight. I just couldn't stand there with her.

She got to the edge and pushed herself up, sweat beading at her temples. "I'm going home."

"Let me give you a ride," I said, still stuck in the pit, not wanting to move.

"Not a chance." She drew herself to her full height. "I think you're really cool, Kiyana. I've had a crush on you for a long time, but I never imagined it looking like this." Her lips trembled before she turned and walked away, her feet heavy on the mats.

My chest ached as I sat there, knowing that once she walked away, she would be gone.

The door slammed shut, and I jerked at the sound. My cue to move. To stop the self-pity. To put on a smile like I'd always been taught to do. Because being yourself got you hurt or hurt someone else.

NINETEEN

XIOMARA

THE SUMMER SUN hit my back but did nothing to cool the ice in my chest. I felt so dumb, not because of what Kiyana had done, but because I hadn't seen it coming. She'd been clear that no one knew about her orientation, and she didn't want them to.

I should have seen our kiss for what it was—she was curious, and I was the person to help give her answers. I just wished that I hadn't liked it so much. That I didn't feel so ashamed right now for giving my first kiss to someone who didn't truly want to be with me. And I wished like hell that I didn't want to kiss her again.

Because not matter how much I denied it, I

wanted someone I could take to the prom. And Kiyana didn't want to go.

I got out my phone and ordered a ride share to take me to the festival. Thankfully a driver was nearby, and I didn't even have to hear Kiyana coming out of the gym before I was driven away.

There were texts on my phone from Van and Shelley asking where I was, asking if Kiyana and I had snuck off somewhere.

I covered my face with my hands, feeling like an even bigger idiot.

Xi: Forget I said anything. I'm on my way there now. Should be there in five.

Shelley: What happened?

Xi: She just wanted to make out with me and move on.

Van: Wait, you made out with her?

Xi: Yes. But nothing more is happening. Ever.

Shelley: We'll meet you in the parking lot.

Then a new message came across my phone.

Unknown Number: Xi, I'm sorry. Can we talk?

Maybe I was a little excited that she had gone to the trouble to acquire my number, but that didn't change the facts. She's not interested in going public with me.

I needed to focus on my friends like I had for

the last year. They had always been there for me, unafraid to be seen with me in public.

The driver slowed in the parking lot, and when I spotted Shelley, Van, and Ronnie, I said, "You can just drop me over there."

He did as I asked, and soon I was out of the car and in Shelley's arms. She hugged me tightly while Van and Ronnie stood to the side and patted my back.

"What happened?" Shelley asked.

I stepped back, wiping moisture from my cheeks. "I was just dumb. I let my feelings get away from me." I was always doing that, so lost in my head I missed what was right in front of me.

Van lightly tapped his fist to my shoulder. "Happens to the best of us."

"Clearly," I teased, conjuring up a smile. "It's okay. I just want to have fun."

Ronnie grinned. "That can be arranged." She glanced at her phone. "We have two hours before we need to be back at your place to get ready for the prom."

"Let's make the most of it," I said, hoping for a distraction strong enough to take my mind off Kiyana and how her lips felt against mine.

TWENTY

KIYANA

I SAT in my car in the empty parking lot, staring at my phone and willing Xi to reply to my text. But nothing came, not even the bubbles to show she was writing or even thinking of me.

Tears stung my eyes, and I took a deep breath, trying to shove them down.

Why did I have to be this way?

Why couldn't I be into boys like all my cheerleading friends were? It looked so easy to them, kissing, holding hands, sitting in the laps of the guys they liked. I would give anything to be the default, but that kiss showed me that I wasn't. And if I ever wanted to feel like that again, I couldn't be.

My phone began ringing, and I snapped it up, hoping that Xi had called so I could apologize, ask for a little more time, but instead Stefon's name was on the screen.

I swiped to answer, taking a deep breath to hide all my hurt, and said, "Hey, Stef."

"Where are you? I just saw Xi with her friends."

I waited for him to fill in the gaps. Say if she looked okay. Happy even. But he waited for my response instead.

"I screwed things up. Already," I said.

"What do you mean?" he asked. I could hear the noise of the festival in the background—laughing and talking and music and games. It couldn't have been more opposite to how I was feeling.

"She asked me to the prom, Stefon."

"Oh my gosh! Did you say yes? Dillon and I were thinking it would be fun to go."

My eyebrows drew together. How could so much have changed in only a day? Stefon was the only person I'd ever been to a dance with, and now he was ready to go public with his boyfriend? "I can't go with her. People would assume I'm gay."

"But you are," he said.

"Stefon..."

"Kiyana, be honest with yourself. You were afraid of having a hard time in high school, but high school is over! The people who matter will be your friends after you come out, and if they aren't, we'll meet tons of people in college who won't care either way!"

I raised my eyebrows. "Why are you making it seem so easy? You saw the way our families reacted!"

"And I'm still standing here." His voice grew gentle. "I know I've only been out for a day, but I can't tell you how good it feels to know I'm not living in hiding anymore. I'm *safe* to be myself in a way I never thought I was before."

Tears rolled down my cheeks, and I wiped them away.

He continued speaking, his voice gentle as ever. "When we started this whole charade, you said you were afraid of getting bullied in high school. High school's over. You said you were afraid of your parents kicking you out. You're living in the dorms, and you have a full-ride scholarship for cheer. You're not going to be homeless, even during summer breaks, because you know you could stay with me. So what is it? What's really holding you back?"

"I don't want my parents to stop loving me!" I let out, my voice echoing around my car. "It might be easy for you to put everything that matters to you at risk, but I'm not as brave as you!"

Stefon was quiet for a moment. "Ki, if they don't love you when they find out you're gay, they never really loved you in the first place. They just loved the version of you they wanted you to be."

It was a punch to the stomach to think the people who birthed me, who raised me, who took me on every family vacation and bought me every birthday present, could stop loving me. Could throw me away.

"What if they don't love me?" I whispered, my voice breaking.

"Your *real* family always will. I'm here for you, Kiyana. Whenever you decide to come out or if you never do. But you deserve to be happy either way."

I sniffed, nodded, even though he couldn't see me. The thought of going to prom with Xi was just as exciting as our kiss had been. But I had so much to lose if I gave into that desire. And unlike Stefon and Xi, I didn't know if I could risk all I had for something new.

XIOMARA

AFTER A DOZEN RIDES down the inflatable slide that did nothing to lighten my mood, we went to my house to get ready for prom. I hadn't been invited to the Emerson Academy junior/senior prom, so this was my first time going to a fancy dance. I would have been excited if not for the hollow ache in my chest.

I'd been so hopeful to have a date, but it wasn't fair of me to ask Kiyana. No one deserved anyone else to come out. I needed to respect her timeline. No matter how much it would suck to be on my own. No matter how much I wanted to kiss her again.

But I had to remember that I wasn't really on

my own. Shelley, Ronnie, and Dee were in my room getting ready while Van hung out in the living room watching TV. Dad and Mom were out helping with festival cleanup before they needed to chaperone tonight. And I knew they were doing that all for me. To help me feel loved and accepted.

From the sounds of it, Kiyana didn't have that. I just hoped, for her sake, that she would someday feel loved as she deserved to be. If Dee wasn't busy applying a sunless tanner to the tank top lines on my shoulders, I would text Kiyana now and apologize for the way I left, for the unfair expectations I'd placed on her.

Shelley sat in a chair as Ronnie worked a large-barreled curling iron through her long blond locks. She smiled over at me and said, "Can you believe we're going to our first prom?"

I shook my head, and Ronnie said, "I can't wait to dance with Van. We've been to Spike together, but it's not the same."

Dee said, "You should enjoy yourselves. I love going out to the clubs and dancing, but it's defi-nitely not the same as a school dance." She giggled. "Everyone wears a lot less clothes, and it gets way colder in Kansas than it does in California."

I laughed at the thought of Dee going to the club with all the other scantily clad college girls. She was our layers girl—always in a hoodie, even in the middle of summer. "Has anyone bedazzled your hoodie yet so you fit in?" I teased.

Dee rolled her eyes. "You need to be nicer to the person putting tanning lotion on you."

"True," I said. It had definitely gone wrong before.

"Do you have a date?" Dee asked Shelley.

Shelley's pale cheeks flushed bright pink. "I do."

"Woo!" Dee cheered. "Tell us about him! Her? They?"

Shelley laughed. "It's a he. He actually goes to Emerson High." Just those few words she spoke about him put a giddy smile on her face.

"What's his name?" Dee asked, already wiping off her hands and reaching for her phone.

"Gunnar Townsend," Shelley answered.

In two seconds flat, Dee had his social media profile on her phone and was scrolling through pictures. I'd already seen photos when Shelley and Gunnar were just talking, but I looked anyway.

"He's cute!" Dee said, flipping through photos of him. He looked like Ken to Shelley's Barbie.

Tall, curly sandy-brown hair, blue eyes, just a few freckles on his cheeks. The perfect match for Shell.

Ronnie nodded. "He's nice too. We all went to Waldo's with him last week, and he was pretty fun to hang out with."

I cringed at the memory of feeling like a fifth wheel the entire time while the couples made moony eyes at each other. I knew they didn't do it on purpose or try to leave me out, but I couldn't help wishing I could have something like that for myself. Someone to hold hands with in the movie theater and kiss when we thought no one was looking.

Ronnie finished running Shelley's hair through the curling iron and sprayed a thick mist of hairspray over the top. Then they swapped places, starting the process on Ronnie's fine brown hair.

"How long have you and Van been dating?" Dee asked her.

With a happy smile, Ronnie said, "We've been together almost nine months, and we haven't even had an argument."

"God, that's an eternity in high school," Dee said. "I'm pretty sure Lucy's longest relationship was three months."

I laughed, remembering feeling like Lucy had a

revolving door of boys coming to pick her up for dates. Dee, on the other hand, had only dated one guy in high school, casually. Part of me had wondered if she might be gay like me, but her new guy had proven my suspicions incorrect.

Maybe I was just like Dee, a late bloomer taking my time to focus on myself and what I wanted. "Do you feel like you missed out on dating in high school?" I asked her.

My friends were silent, seeming just as interested in her answer as I was.

Dee took a breath, leaning back against my desk as she thought it over. "I used to wish and wish that guys would notice me like they did my friends. I remember going to dances like this and focusing so much on how I looked to the guys there, whether I was holding my chin the right way or if there was enough of a smile on my lips. Now that I am dating, I wish I wouldn't have spent so much time worrying about things that didn't matter. I should have been focusing on my friends, on having fun, on figuring out who I really was." She shrugged. "Boyfriends are great, and I like mine"—she gave a sheepish grin—"but at the same time, it's not like there's a checklist for a successful high school experience. You get to decide what it is for you."

I nodded, feeling relief. She was right. Maybe now was my time for friendship, for self-discovery, for fun with my parents. And yeah, there was plenty of homework to keep me busy too. And now that I knew what it felt like to kiss a girl, I had that much more to look forward to.

We finished applying makeup, and soon it was time to put on our outfits. Shelley had this pretty dark blue dress that had crisscross straps across her back. Ronnie had opted for a suit made of purple velvet with an oversized blazer and a lacy bandeau underneath. Dee got into a pink prom dress she'd worn her senior year, with sheer sleeves and a plunging neckline that showed off all her curves.

And then I got my dress from the hanger.

I pulled the layers of tulle over my head, sliding into my gorgeous lime-green dress. The color contrasted beautifully with my tanned skin, and the sparkles caught the light even in my bedroom. I couldn't wait to see how it would look under the disco ball we'd set up.

We helped each other with zippers and buttons and ties and hair touch-ups, and soon we were walking down the stairs.

At the sound of our footsteps, Van looked up from the TV, and his lip piercing glinted in the light as he smiled. "Well now I look like a schmuck," he said, standing to take us in.

"You do not," Ronnie argued. "You look very handsome." He'd worn a retro suit himself with a fluffy cummerbund. But now I noticed something in his hands.

"I got this for you," he said to Ronnie, opening the plastic box. Inside was a corsage with two rainbow roses and beautifully arranged ribbon.

My lips parted in shock as I took in how beautiful it was.

Ronnie smiled wide, holding her hands to her chest. "It's perfect, Van."

He grinned, flipping his black hair out of his eyes. "May I?"

She nodded and extended her arm to him. He easily slid the band over her wrist and adjusted the flowers just so. With it on, she bent her elbow, bringing the flowers to her nose and breathing deeply. "Perfect," she said.

From behind me, Dee said, "Let's get some pictures before we have to go!"

I nodded. "Let's do it outside on the steps. It'll be fun to pose there with all Mom's decorations."

Shelley laughed. "They should put the house in the June issue of *Better Homes and Gardens*."

"Agreed," Ronnie said, slipping her fingers through Van's.

My eyes trailed to their linked hands, sadness and envy sweeping over me. Only hours ago, I'd held Kiyana's hand and felt so much more than I knew I could. I hoped Van and Ronnie didn't take that simple gesture for granted, not even for a minute.

Ahead of me, Shelley said, "What is this?"

Ronnie squealed. "Oh my gosh! You got us a limo?"

I glanced to Dee and then followed my friends outside to see a white stretch limo parked along the curb, engine running and driver standing by the door.

Dee grinned, saying, "Surprise from Mom and Dad."

My friends cheered and I hugged Dee, not believing they had gone to all this trouble for me.

"They love you so much," Dee said.

My eyes stung at the truth in her words. "We're so lucky to have them."

She nodded. "You have no idea."

"Actually, I think I do." We smiled at each other for a moment, and Dee said, "You four get in front of the limo so I can have a picture of you all!"

We posed in front of the vehicle, taking tons of pictures, while the driver waited. I knew I'd be printing all of them and hanging them in my locker next year. I wanted to remember just how happy and loved I felt in this moment, with or without a date.

TWENTY-TWO

KIYANA

I SAT in the driveway to my house, looking through the front window. With the curtains open, I could see Grandma knitting away. Mom sat in the recliner, a hardcover book in her lap. She never read any other kind of book. Dad and Grandpa weren't there, probably doing something in the backyard. The climbing rose bushes were like his second child.

Tears stung my eyes as I realized this could be the last time. The last time my grandparents ever came to visit while I was here. The last time my parents saw me as just Kiyana.

The last time my mom ever assumed she'd have grandbabies the way she imagined.

The last time they looked at me without disappointment or shame.

Maybe the last time they looked at me at all.

Because whether I told them now or a year from now or even ten years from now, it wouldn't change the truth of who I was. And Stefon was right; if they didn't love all of me, they didn't love any of me.

Mom glanced up from her book and saw me through the window. She waved me in, and I nodded, barely managing a smile. My legs and arms felt robotic as they carried me out of the car, toward the place I'd called home my entire life.

Mom opened the door for me, letting me in as she asked, "How was your time with the girls?"

She and Grandma seemed expectant for my answer, but if I was going to be honest, I needed to start now. "Actually, I went to see Stefon. He has a new boyfriend."

Mom's eyes widened. "What?"

Grandma sputtered. "Was he dating someone else before he ended things with you?"

I looked between the two of them, guarding my heart for what would come next. "He met a guy who goes to the college we'll be attending, and I guess they hit it off."

Grandma's hands worked furiously through the blanket she was knitting, but I kept my eyes trained on Mom, trying to read her expression. She seemed more conflicted than anything else. "I mean, I'm glad he's happy," she finally said.

"Happy?" Grandma scoffed. "It's not about being happy. It's about doing what is *right*."

I gritted my teeth. "You mean by not cheating on me?" I hoped that was what she meant, although I should have known better.

She gave me a look. "I've never been to a wedding at the church between two men."

I closed my eyes, and Mom let out a quiet sigh.

"Things are different now, Mama," she said. "And just because he's with someone else doesn't mean all Kiyana's feelings are gone right away. She clearly still cares for him deeply."

I stared at my mom, in disbelief that she was standing up for Stefon to my grandma. If I had learned one thing from my parents, it was that you never talked back to your elders, never questioned them.

"Things may be different, but that doesn't mean better," Grandma said. "As far as I'm concerned, you're better off without him in your life, Kiyana."

Mom tilted her head. "What if Kiyana said she

was gay? Would you just write her off?" Now I noticed the tears in my mom's eyes. Felt how close I was to crying myself.

Grandma gave Mom a long, slow look, then stood up and said, "I'm going to draw me a bath."

We were silent as Grandma took her time walking away, but I gave Mom a questioning look.

"I talked to his mother today," Mom said quietly, tears in her eyes. "She was so scared for him. Did you know that last year one in four gay teens attempted suicide? *Twenty-five percent* had the idea it was better to die than be alive." She shifted her gaze to the back bedroom where Grandma had gone. "I know it comes from comments like that. Like feeling that they're not good enough or there's something wrong with them."

My chest felt tight, and I could hardly breathe. "So Stefon's parents... they're supporting him?"

Mom nodded. "What else can they do? Lose their son?" She pressed her fingertips to the corners of her eyes. "There is no other choice. Not when you love your children the way we do."

We? I opened my mouth, and all the words tumbled out. "Mom, I'm a lesbian... I like girls." I covered my chest with my hands, feeling like if I didn't, my heart would fall out of my chest. "I needed to tell you before I moved away."

But she looked at me like she was seeing me for the first time. "How long have you known?"

My voice cracked. "Since seventh grade."

Mom covered her mouth with her hand, her eyes flitting side to side as she saw memories I couldn't. All the comments made at church when we went with my grandparents. All the jokes made at gay people's expense. Every word like a thousand paper cuts doused in lemon juice.

"Five years," she whispered. "And you and Stefon? You dated that whole time?"

"We were there for each other," I said, tears falling down my cheeks. "We didn't want to disappoint anyone."

She choked on a sob, extending her arms to me. My legs carried me toward her, and she held me tighter than she ever had before. "You could never disappoint me, baby. You're my only daughter. My only child." She pulled back, holding my face in her hands, a look of wonder in her eyes. "You're my baby."

Tears fell quickly down my cheeks. Tears of relief. Of gratitude. Of love.

"I love you, Mom."

She held me again. "I love you so much."

We stayed like that for a long time, just rocking back and forth, holding each other until the back door opened and Dad and Grandpa came inside.

Mom cleared her throat and said, "Daryl, we need to talk to you. Sorry, Daddy, we need a minute."

Grandpa nodded and said, "A catnap sounds good to me." He patted Dad's back and walked to the bedroom where Grandma had gone.

Taking in Mom and me, Dad's expression quickly grew concerned. "Is everything okay?"

Mom nodded and looked to me. "Do you want to tell him?"

No, but Mom's reaction had given me enough safety. Even if I lost my dad, I'd have her. "Dad, I'm a lesbian. Stefon and I, we've been pretending to be together so no one would bully us. So I wouldn't lose your love."

A crease grew between his eyebrows as he looked between Mom and me. Mom nodded, and he scrubbed his face with his hand. "Ki—I mean, I had no idea." His voice was hoarse with emotion.

"How could you?" I asked, my lip trembling. "It was all I could do to keep the secret. But it's been crushing me in ways I didn't even fully understand until today."

"What happened today?" he asked.

I looked between him and Mom, a smile touching my lips despite all the fear I'd felt only moments ago. "I met someone. And she asked me to the pride prom."

Mom glanced toward the clock. "It's almost seven... When does it start?"

My smile fell. "I didn't even think to ask. I didn't know if I'd be allowed."

Dad said, "Allowed? Kiyana, you're an adult now. It comes with some extra responsibilities, but it also comes with freedom to do what you want with your life. We can't choose that for you. Only you're in charge of that."

Mom nodded. "You'll make mistakes and learn a lot, but Daddy and I will always be here for you, no matter what."

All the pieces of my heart I hadn't even known had been broken came together in that moment. I was loved, seen, in every way. But there was something none of us had mentioned. The elephant in the room—or rather the guest bedroom. "What about Grandma and Grandpa?"

Mom and Dad exchanged a look, and Mom

took my face in her hands. "You are our family. If they can't accept you, they don't need to be a part of it."

"But Mom—" I hated the idea of losing them.

She shook her head. "One in four, Kiyana. I will *not* let you be one of them. We will *not* have people around who make you feel like you are worth less than what you deserve. And, baby girl, you deserve the world."

My jaw trembled, and I hugged her hard. "I love you."

"We love you too," Mom said.

Dad said, "Now, don't you have a prom to get to? I don't want you to miss it."

I smiled up at him, wiping my eyes. "Thank you. I'll go get ready now."

I just hoped when I arrived, my date would be happy to see me too.

TWENTY-THREE

XIOMARA

WHEN THE LIMO pulled in front of the school, I couldn't help but notice how full the parking lot was. We'd expected maybe fifty to a hundred people, but judging by the amount of cars spilling out along the street, there had to be at least double that.

My heart swelled with pride, and I said to my friends, "I hope everyone likes our decorations."

Dee put her hand on my arm. "They're going to love them."

"Yeah," Van agreed. "Ollie and I spent way too long on that ceiling gossamer for anyone to complain."

I laughed. "You make a good point."

The limo slowed along the curb, and the driver

called back, "Is everyone ready, or shall I make another loop?"

Dee squeezed my hand, and I nodded. "We're ready."

He stopped the vehicle and got out to hold open the door. Shelley got out first and ran to meet Gunnar, who was waiting for her at the bench. He took her in his arms and spun her around in the cutest way.

Then Van climbed out of the limo and held Ronnie's hand as she stepped out. They looked like they were ready to strut the red carpet. And then it was Dee and me.

She squeezed my hand. "I know you're sad not to have a date, but just remember, you're never alone." She tapped my nose. "Not with our crazy family."

I laughed, holding her hand back. "Have I mentioned that Kansas is too far?"

"You're starting to sound like Mom," she teased, getting up. "Come on. Let's see all of your hard work come to life."

I followed her out of the car and took in every moment. The dimming light in the sky, the warm breeze playing softly across my shoulders, the swish of dresses as we walked over the sidewalk with the rest of the people going to the prom.

I didn't even recognize most everyone walking into Emerson Academy, which made me excited. This pride event, it was bigger than me, bigger than Emerson. And even though some people had to hide, I hoped we could honor them by being our truest selves tonight.

At the top of the stairs, Dee pulled the door open for me, but I said, "You go in. I need a minute."

She nodded, giving me a gentle smile before heading inside.

I stood at the railing, overlooking the school courtyard. I had two more years at Emerson Academy, but I mourned for the four years Stefon and Kiyana had spent keeping secrets. And even though I couldn't understand, even though I hadn't been through the same experience, I felt for them.

I went back to the message thread with Kiyana. It was time to write her back.

Xiomara: Kiyana, I had an incredible time getting to know you. It was more fun than I ever could have imagined. And I can't tell you how sorry I am for trying to pressure you into coming out. You don't owe anyone your truth until you're ready to share it. So no matter how much I wish I could twirl with you under the disco ball, I hope you know that today was and will always be enough. I hope you have the very best time at college, and I know your life will be just as incredible as you are.

I hit send and put my phone on silent before placing it back in my clutch. I was going to follow Dee's advice and stop worrying so much about what I was missing out on. Because I had great friends who loved me, parents who would do anything for me, and a prom to enjoy.

I followed a couple inside the school and walked to the gym, where the hum of voices and soft music blended to a dull roar. A photographer had set up by the boat, taking photos of couples. Servers walked about, carrying trays of non-alcoholic drinks for everyone to enjoy.

And then I saw my parents standing together in black clothes, rainbow chaps, and matching cowboy hats.

I let out a giggle as I saw them, Dad's arm around Mom's waist. I hoped I could have a love like theirs someday. A family like ours.

Dad caught sight of me first and waved me over. "Xi, you look stunning," he said.

Mom smiled, her eyes moist for the millionth time today. "You are absolutely beautiful."

I did a spin, loving the way I felt in my dress, surrounded by people who cared so deeply for me. "I feel beautiful."

Mom said, "Will you go take a picture with the photographer? I already filled out a form for you and Dee so we can get copies."

"Sure, I'll take a picture, but only if you and Dad will take one with me?"

Dad laughed. "I guess this outfit is going down in history."

Mom nodded, reaching for his hand. "How could we forget what a great dad you are?"

I spotted Dee and called her over, and we made our way through the crowd. At the boat, the photographer posed us. Dee and me in the middle and our parents on either side.

The flash went off, freezing this moment, our love, forever.

A deep voice came over the speaker system, saying, "I'm DJ Dance, and I'm here to get this party started!"

Cheering sounded all around us, and we clapped along.

"Let's start this prom off right with a good old-fashioned slow dance," DJ Dance said.

Everyone clapped as a country song began

playing over the speakers. Dad held his cowboy hat to his chest, asking Mom to dance in a corny southern accent. Dee and I giggled, but as soon as she said yes, he spun her away to the slowly growing throng of couples.

"They're so cute," Dee said.

"Agreed," I replied. "And since neither of us has a date... Will you be my first dance?"

Dee glanced over my shoulder, and then I heard Kiyana say, "Actually, I was hoping you would dance with me."

TWENTY-FOUR

KIYANA

XI SLOWLY TURNED TOWARD ME. Her mouth formed a question to match her eyes, but no sound came out.

Dee nudged her sister. As if that was all Xi needed to snap out of her surprise, she nodded, her throat moving as she swallowed. "I'll dance with you."

I extended my hand and watched as her fingers landed in mine, the perfect match, perfect contrast to my own.

We walked a few steps closer to the center of the gym where other couples of every gender, age, and color were dancing together. It felt like a huge win, but I wasn't so sure whether I should be celebrating yet. Xi had seemed so hurt earlier, and her text had brought me to tears before coming in here.

"Hey," she said, a small smile on her lips.

The relief that simple word brought me made me smile. "Hey."

She tilted her head to the side. "Can I ask the obvious question?"

I nodded, still feeling breathless from all the events of the day.

"How did you get here?"

"I drove."

She laughed, the sound pure music to my ears. "Really," she said. "Does anyone know you came?"

"After you left the tumbling gym, I went home, frustrated about all I was missing out on. I loved my high school experience. Stefon was the best fake boyfriend, and I had a great time on the cheerleading squad. But today showed me that I want more. And I could only think of one way to do that."

Xi's smile touched every corner of her face. It was just as intoxicating as her kiss had been. "And your parents were okay with it?"

Tears stung my eyes at the memory of my parents. How supportive they'd been. "They said they love me no matter what and even said they would stand up to my grandparents for me." I removed my hand from her shoulder to wipe my eyes before my makeup could be ruined. "I have to thank Stefon. Our moms spoke earlier today, and I think him taking the step first made it easier for me."

She let go of my hand and put her arms around me for too short of a hug, our dance forgotten altogether. "Kiyana, I'm so happy for you!"

When she stepped back, I kept my arms linked around her neck so we could dance a little closer. I liked looking at her this close up. Her eyes were the prettiest almond shape, and her eyebrows were sharp and strong, the perfect contrast to her full, soft lips.

I wanted to kiss her again. But there would be time.

God, I was so thankful there would be time.

"You look beautiful tonight," Xi said.

My cheeks were warm as I glanced down at my dress. The white knee-length gown was a gift from my mom. She'd found it one day shopping, and since plus-size stores were always in short supply of anything worthwhile, she snagged it up. It was as if the universe knew I'd be here today with Xi and wanted me to look my best.

Xi, on the other hand, stole the entire night. Her lime-green gown spilled around her until it tickled the floor. Each sequin and shimmer in the tulle skirt caught the light from the disco ball. She was stunning, absolutely captivating.

The song drew to a close, and I frowned. I wanted to keep dancing.

Xi giggled and said, "There will be another slow song."

The flush came quickly, but so did my smile. "I hope you'll dance it with me."

She took my hands, swaying side to side with the new song. "Like I'm letting you dance with anyone else."

I grinned, taking in the moment, rejoicing in the scary, exciting feeling of being out with a girl in public for the first time in my life.

And then someone brushed my arm. I looked over to apologize and saw Stefon standing beside me.

"What are you doing here?" he asked over the music. He glanced around at the people dancing around us. "Aren't you worried people will see you?"

Shaking my head, I said, "Not anymore! My

parents both know, and everything is going to be okay."

He hugged me tight, taking me away from Xi so he could pick me up and spin me in a circle. "I'm so proud of you!"

Smiling up at him, I said, "It is pride, is it not?"

He took my hand and twirled me. "You're incredible."

"And so are you." I reached up and held his face in my hands. "I couldn't have gotten through high school without you, and I couldn't have told my parents what I did today without seeing you do it first."

"You always had it in you," he replied, then stepped back. "And now we get to celebrate it."

Xi and Dillon joined hands with us, dancing and jumping with the music. Never before had I felt so free.

Never before had I felt so *me*.

XIOMARA

MY DAD ASKED me to dance the next slow song with him, and even though I wanted nothing more than to keep my arms around Kiyana all night, I couldn't turn him down. The guy had come to the prom in rainbow chaps, after all.

He took my hand in his and then put one on my back, spinning me around the dance floor. Dad was an excellent dancer, having learned merengue and salsa and even the waltz under his mother's tutelage. For now though, we just moved to the music, enjoying each other's company.

"I saw you dancing with Kiyana," he said, a sly smile on his face.

My cheeks instantly grew hot and I looked away to hide my smile. "What about it?"

"You look happy, Xi," he said.

I smiled up at him. "I am. I mean, it's not that I wasn't before, but it all feels...fresh."

"I get it. Romance is one of the best parts of life, and I'm happy you're getting to experience it."

I nodded, glancing over our hands to see Kiyana and Stefon dancing together. I wondered how I had never noticed it before—the fact that they interacted like friends instead of lovers. Most people dating in our school danced with their bodies pressed up against each other, but she and Stefon had always left more than enough room.

"She's leaving for college tomorrow," I said. "I barely got to know her at all, and now she's gone."

Dad smiled down at me. "You know they have these newfangled things now called cell phones. You can talk and send messages and—"

"You know it's not the same," I replied with a roll of my eyes.

"Maybe not. But that school's only an hour and a half away, and Mom and I have been talking about getting a new car..."

My jaw dropped. "You're saying I could have Mom's old car?"

He nodded. "You've passed your driving test already, and no matter how much I hate to admit it, you're growing up. We're just lucky to have a front row seat."

I squeezed him, thanking him. Maybe things wouldn't work out with Kiyana and me long-term, but the fact that I had freedom, possibilities, that was more than enough for me.

The song came to a close, and Dad gave me another hug. "Enjoy your night, kiddo. We want you home by two."

"Two?" I asked, not believing I'd have a whole two hours after the dance was over to spend with my friends, and hopefully, with Kiyana.

He gave me a wink. "Be safe."

My friends approached me, Shelley and Gunnar holding hands and Van's arm around Ronnie's waist.

Ronnie said, "Looks like you got your happily ever after after all."

Kiyana came and slipped her fingers through mine. "I know I did."

TWENTY-SIX

KIYANA

I LOVED DANCING WITH XIOMARA, but I wanted her to myself. Around midnight, I got my wish.

The last song faded to a close, and the gym lights turned on, taking away all the magic of the disco ball. All good things had to come to an end, and I felt the clock ticking now more than ever. I wished I could stay in Emerson longer, wished I didn't have to leave for college so soon. But I knew I'd be coming back to visit, and now I had even more to return for.

Xi and I broke apart, walking to join our friends in a haphazard circle. Our hair was slightly less perfect, and the guys had ditched their blazers somewhere in the night, but everyone was smiling.

"What's next?" Xi asked.

Dillon said, "I wish I could hang out longer, but I need to start driving back home."

Stefon nodded. "I'll walk you out." He gave me a subtle wink before linking hands with his boyfriend and moving toward the door.

Shelley said, "Gunnar was going to take me for milkshakes at Waldo's. Anyone want to join us?"

Van glanced at Ronnie, and they nodded in unison. "We'll go," Ronnie said. They looked at us, waiting for our answer. I turned to Xi, silently begging her to spend my last night in town with only me.

Her cheeks were the most adorable shade of peach as she said, "I'm going to hang out with Ki."

Shelley's mouth fell open, and she put her free hand over her heart. "Oh my gosh, that's so adorable! Xi and Ki!"

Xi rolled her eyes as if she weren't grinning just as happily as I was.

"Come on," I said, squeezing her hand.

She tightened her grip on mine, and as we walked away, her friends wolf-whistled and catcalled at us. I couldn't get my smile to go away or even dim as every eye fell on me and the most beautiful girl in the room.

We walked out the gym doors, down the hall-way, and outside. A gust of warm air fluttered the bottom of my dress, and I held it down just in case. "I wish I had a long dress like yours to keep me modest."

She grinned. "I like seeing your legs. Reminds me of your cheerleading uniform." She winked.

I stared at her, stalling at the top of the stairs with a surprised smile on my lips. "You were watching me?"

"How could I not?" She squeezed my hand. "You have a tendency to draw the eyes. I just never knew anything could be possible between us."

I was silent, taking it in. Wondering just how long she had noticed me. How long we could have been holding hands before now.

"Did you ever notice me?" she asked shyly.

I reached up, carefully tucking a flyaway strand of hair behind her ear. "I couldn't. Because if I looked too long, I wouldn't have been able to keep up the act. You're magnetic, Xiomara Muñoz."

She shivered slightly against my touch. "I'm having trouble staying away myself."

"Then kiss me," I said, my voice blending with the wind.

Even in the dim lighting, the surprise was clear on her face. "Here? With everyone walking by?"

I nodded. Dancing with her in public was one thing, but to stand here, on the steps of my old high school where I had spent so much time hiding parts of myself… A kiss with Xiomara felt like poetic justice. Like destiny. Like *Ad Meliora*.

She stepped closer, the tulle of her dress brushing against my bare legs. And then her hand reached to my cheek.

Our eyes locked. One final chance to back away.

But I leaned in, kissing her exactly the way I wanted to. Long, slow, tender, and absolutely carefree of who would see us and what they would think.

I was never going back. Only forward, and hopefully with this beautiful girl at my side.

TWENTY-SEVEN

XIOMARA

KIYANA and I parted just long enough to walk to her car, and since I didn't want my parents to see us fogging the windows, I asked her to drive. To where, I had no idea.

She didn't want me at her house with her homophobic grandparents around, and the last thing I needed was my parents smothering us with their support. I loved them, but nothing stopped sparks from flying like snacks hand-delivered to your room at one in the morning.

Kiyana glanced at me with a smile. "I have an idea."

I knew we both liked surprises, so I sat quietly beside her, listening to her upbeat music and holding her hand as she drove away from the school.

Several minutes later, she parked in the empty lot to Emerson Trails and glanced over to me. "Care to attend the festival as my date?"

I let out a laugh. "Everything is taken down already."

"We can pretend."

"Sure," I said, getting out of the car. Kiyana went to the trunk and pulled out a blanket she kept there, and we walked in our dresses toward the dimly lit sidewalk. I shucked my heels to make walking down the sloping grass easier, and Kiyana did the same, slipping her sandal straps through her fingers.

"What was it like earlier?" she asked. "At the festival?"

I pointed to the spot where the inflatable slide had been. "There was a massive inflatable there. Someone stood at the top passing out gunny sacks, and then we'd slide down on our bellies. It was tall enough to be fun but not too tall to be scary."

She quirked an eyebrow. "And you didn't trip?"

I stuck my tongue out at her, and she laughed.

"Ollie, Birdie's stepson, had a stand over there

selling plants and rainbow roses. He says if you cut the stems and put them in different colored water, the colors will come up to the petals."

"They sound beautiful," Kiyana said.

"They were." I found myself wishing I would have gotten one for her, regardless of how things worked out. "And then of course there was a food truck selling funnel cakes, and this place called Seaton Bakery had the most delicious confetti cupcakes with rainbow frosting and little pride flags."

"I haven't been there before, but I'll have to go when I'm back in town... maybe you'll come with me?"

The hope in her voice made my heart soar. Maybe this wasn't just a one-night thing after all. Maybe there could be a future for us and not just a past. "Of course I'll go with you," I said.

She squeezed my hand, and we walked a little farther. "The only thing that was missing from the festival was you," I said.

She smiled at me, brightening even the darkest parts of the night. "Want to sit here and look at the stars?"

I nodded, despite only wanting to see the stars in her eyes.

She spread the blanket out and lifted it until it fluttered gently to the ground. The gray material was dark against the grass, and her white dress contrasted it all as she lay down. I adjusted my long skirt and lay beside her.

This close to her, I was strangely self-conscious of my chin, my chest, how I looked lying flat. But those worries quickly faded away as she reached for my hand.

We lay together, looking up at the stars dotting the sky.

"My favorite constellation is Orion." She pointed, and I followed her finger to the three stars of his belt.

"Why is that your favorite?" I asked. To me, picking a favorite star in the sky was like choosing a favorite grain of sand.

"I think I related to the fight, always struggling against myself."

"And how do you feel now?"

She rolled her head to the side, smiling at me. "Excited."

"For college?" I asked, trying not to get my hopes up.

But she reached out, brushing her fingers across my cheek. "For this." She drew closer, pressing her lips against mine. And then she whispered, "And every moment after."

TWENTY-EIGHT

KIYANA

I MAY HAVE ONLY SLEPT six hours, but I felt more energized than ever. Every time I closed my eyes, I pictured Xi. Saw her dark eyes smiling at me. Felt her lips against mine. Grew excited at the memory of her fingertips trailing over my skin. I had to see her, one more time before I left.

When the sun came creeping through my windows, I got out of bed, took a shower to wash off the makeup and stray pieces of grass from the night before. Then I took my time putting on fresh makeup and doing my hair for my first day on campus. For my hopeful date with Xi.

I didn't want to wake her up, but I couldn't wait anymore, so I got out my phone and sent her a message.

Kiyana: Can I take you out for a cupcake at Seaton Bakery? I want to see you before I go.

Within minutes, I had my answer.

Xi: What time?

Kiyana: How about two hours from now?

Xi: I'll be there. Can't wait. :)

Still smiling, I put my phone in the pocket of my leggings (because who has time for leggings without pockets anymore) and went out to the kitchen. My dad sat at the counter, sipping from a cup of coffee ,and Mom stood over the stove, stirring a pan of scrambled eggs.

"Morning," I said. "It smells incredible in here."

They smiled at me, so much feeling in their expressions.

"Thanks," Mom said.

"How was the prom?" Dad asked.

"It was the best prom I've ever been to. Stefon was there too, with his boyfriend."

Mom turned, still holding the spatula. "That's good. I'm glad you two are going to be there for each other through all the new firsts."

I nodded, sliding into the bar stool next to Dad. I felt so relieved to know I could sit with them and fully be myself. Now I understood why Stefon had looked so light after he came out. I felt it too, with every breath I took. But there was still one thing I worried about. "How did Grandma and Grandpa take the news?"

Mom and Dad exchanged a look, and my stomach dropped. "What happened?"

Dad put his hand over mine. "They were a little surprised at first, but we came to an agreement. They will be in our lives, only if they do not question yours or make you feel any less deserving of love than you are." He cupped my cheek with his hand. "They love you, even if they don't understand everything right now."

I held his hand to my cheek. It wasn't perfect—it was life. And I was glad I had a few good people in my corner. "Thanks, Dad."

Mom set a plate of eggs and toast with butter and jelly in front of me. "Eat up. You have a big day."

I took a bite and shared the news that made today even bigger. "I'm going to meet Xi for lunch before I go."

Mom folded her hands over her heart. "I actually texted her mom last night... You're looking at the newest members of the Emerson Pride Association!"

I looked between her and Dad. "For real?"

Dad nodded. "Guess you'll have to come back for the prom next year. I heard it was a big hit." He winked.

Shaking my head, I continued eating the rest of my breakfast, thankful for my parents and excited for everything that was to come.

It took the three of us a little more than an hour to pack my car to the brim with everything I'd bring to college. It took a little less than that to say good-bye. There were hugs and tears and words of encouragement. But most of all, there was hope. Hope that the next chapter in my life would be the best one yet.

XIOMARA

I PULLED MOM'S—MY—CAR into Seaton Bakery's gravel parking lot. From the outside, you wouldn't think much of the place. It had dingy white paint and window markers announcing a breakfast special of a muffin and coffee for four dollars.

To be fair, the appearance didn't really matter. Not when Kiyana would be meeting me here. Not when I had all the jitters of a new relationship to go with the disappointment of a premature goodbye.

As soon as I had turned off the vehicle and opened the door, I saw Kiyana's car hit the lot. Heard the pop of gravel under her tires. She looked adorable in a white hoodie framed by moving boxes in the back and passenger seats. Another reminder of what was to come.

Her engine quieted, and she got out of the car, offering me a smile and a "Hey."

I worried things would be awkward between us with the relationship being so new, but it was as natural as breathing to run up to her and give her a hug. She kissed my lips for far too short and then slipped her fingers through mine.

"Do you think they have any pride cupcakes left?" she asked.

"If we're lucky," I replied.

We walked through the door to jingling bells, our fingers still linked. A woman behind the counter grinned at us. "Aren't you two just the cutest couple!" My cheeks warmed, but she continued, looking at me. "I saw you at the festival yesterday. My name's Gayle."

"Hi, Gayle," Kiyana said. "I'm Kiyana." She extended her hand over the counter, and they shook. Kiyana was a natural around other people. It took me just a little bit longer to warm up, but I smiled and said, "Hi, I'm Xiomara. But everyone calls me Xi."

"What can I get you two?" Gayle asked.

While I scanned the display case, Kiyana said,

"Do you have any cupcakes left from the festival yesterday? Xi told me how amazing they are."

Gayle grinned. "I actually have a few left. I wasn't going to sell them since they aren't fresh, but if you want one, you can have it on the house!"

"Awesome!" Kiyana said. "Can I have that and a chicken salad sandwich with a lemonade?"

Gayle rang it up, and then I asked for a sandwich with a little extra spice. We carried our drinks and desserts back to a corner booth, and within minutes, Gayle had all of our food out. This place was already becoming my new favorite.

"What are you thinking?" Kiyana asked.

I realized I'd been so lost in my thoughts I hadn't spoken for a little bit. "I was actually just thinking about how at home I feel here."

"I know," she agreed, looking around. "It's not flashy, but it's comfy. We'll have to come here next time I'm in town."

I raised my eyebrows, surprised and more than a little pleased about her plans for the future. "You want to meet up next time you're here?"

Kiyana smiled, nudging my foot under the table. "Why wouldn't I?"

I looked down at the table for a moment, afraid of messing up my best and only relationship. "My three sisters always talked about college like it's this fun time to explore and figure out who you are. I wouldn't want to take that from you."

When I built up the courage to meet her eyes, she was smiling gently. "Xi, you've taught me more about myself and given me more adventure in twenty-four hours than I've had in eighteen years." Her foot nudged mine again, sending tingles up my leg. "I don't want to lose the opportunity to find out what this could be."

My smile was so big, I must have looked like a cartoon character. "Are you sure?"

She nodded. "Actually..." She reached into her purse and got out an envelope, passing it to me. I opened it, seeing tickets to the Indigo Girls, along with fifty dollars. "I was hoping I could take you to the concert. If you're interested."

I grinned, looking at the date of the concert and imprinting it on my heart. "I'd love to go with you!"

"Good." She gave a satisfied smile, then took a bite of her chicken salad sandwich, letting out a little moan. "It's so good."

My food was delicious too, but I was pretty sure anything would taste sweet with all these butterflies dancing in my stomach, lapping up every moment.

We stayed at the table, eating our food, drinking

lemonade, savoring every bite of cupcake and every moment we had together. But eventually our time, this whirlwind weekend, had to come to an end.

We walked outside to her car, putting off the inevitable goodbye. I thought of the tickets in my purse, remembering it was really just a "see you later."

She held both of my hands in hers, looking from our linked fingers to my eyes. "I don't feel like thank you is enough, Xi."

"Don't thank me," I replied, wishing the best day of my summer wasn't coming to an end already. "You're amazing, Kiyana. You would have figured it out without me."

"But it's better with you." She cupped my cheek and pressed her lips to mine. I loved the way she tasted, like sugar and mint and possibilities. She drew back far too soon and said, "Call me, okay?"

I nodded, stepping back so she could get in her car. She sat down and shut the door, the punctuation mark on a whirlwind romance I never expected or even knew I could hope for.

And then she backed out, giving me a final flutter of her fingers before driving away.

I held back tears as her vehicle disappeared around a corner and I walked back to my car.

Wiping at my eyes, I got in and pulled out the concert tickets. They were a promise of what was to come.

And then my phone began ringing over the car speakers. I looked to the radio screen and smiled.

Incoming call from Kiyana.

As I answered her call, I knew one thing for sure. This wasn't the end. It was only the beginning.

Want to see the inspiration behind Curvy Girls Can't Date Curvy Girls? Visit kelsiestelting.com/pride!

GLOSSARY

LATIN PHRASES

Ad Meliora: School motto meaning "toward better things."

Audentes fortuna iuvat: Motto of *Dulce Periculum* meaning "Fortune favors the bold."

Dulce Periculum: means "danger is sweet" - local secret club that performs stunts

Multum in Parvo: means "much in little"

LOCATIONS

Town Name: Emerson

Location: Halfway between Los Angeles and San Francisco

Surrounding towns: Brentwood, Seaton, Heywood

Emerson Academy: Private school Rory and Beckett attend

Brentwood Academy: Rival private school

Walden Island: Tourism island off the coast, only accessible by helicopter or ferry

Laughlin: Small country between England and Scotland formed in the early 1900s.

MacColl: Capital city of Laughlin where the royal family resides.

MAIN HANGOUTS

Emerson Elementary Library: Where Rory tutors Anna, open to students K-7

Emerson Field: Massive park in the center of Emerson

Emerson Memorial: Local hospital

Emerson Shoppes: Shopping mall

Emerson Trails: Hiking trails in Emerson, near Emerson Field

Halfway Café: Expensive dining option in Emerson, frequented by celebrities

La La Pictures: Movie theater in Emerson

Ripe: Major health food store serving the tri-city area

Roasted: Popular coffee shop in Emerson

JJ Cleaning: Cleaning service owned by Jordan's mom

Seaton Bakery: Delicious dining and drink option in Seaton where Beckett works

Seaton Beach: Beach near Seaton – rougher than the beach near Brentwood

Seaton Pier: Fishing pier near Seaton

Spike's: Local 18-and-under club

Waldo's Diner: local diner, especially popular after sporting events

APPS

Rush+: Game app designed by Kai Rush and his father

Sermo: chat app used by private school students

IMPORTANT ENTITIES

Bhatta Productions: Production company owned by Zara's father

Brentwood Badgers: Professional football team

Heywood Market: Big ranch/distributor where everyone can purchase their meat locally

Invisible Mountains: Local major nonprofit - Callie's dad is the CEO

Dugan Industries: Owns and manages Brentwood Marina, along with other entities. Owned by Ryker Dugan's father, Trent Dugan.

I grew up in a small midwestern town where crosses line the highways and school lessons on topics like evolution are filled with "well if you believe that..." and "what really happened is..." All sporting events were preceded with team prayers, and no one hung out on Sunday mornings because that was church time.

And I swallowed every word. Believed every lie.

In my heart, I thought I was doing what was required to be a "good girl" in the eyes of God. I thought I would earn my salvation and demonstrate the fruits of the spirit by rejecting things old men in elaborate garb called sin.

Never mind the sin that separated me from

other humans, the sin that leads people to believe they are not enough in the eyes of God.

And then I graduated high school and moved away and joined the world—the real world full of people with different origins, different backgrounds, different beliefs. And it was beautiful, wonderful, colorful in a way my youth had never been.

Hanging on to dogma became exhausting. Separating myself from others didn't feel right. My faith in these old beliefs was wavering...

And then I adopted children.

When I look into the eyes of my babies, I see love. I see their souls, gentle and kind and learning to navigate a world that isn't always those things. And I know, deep within my own soul, that nothing could change that love I have for them. Especially not if they were gay. Especially not if they were happy and in love. The last thing I would want is for them to be afraid of me, of the divine.

And as that truth dawned on me, I looked back in horror at all I had done and said around different sexual orientations. I hated the support I gave to unaffirming organizations. I imagined growing up queer in a small town that espoused the evils of homosexuality and made jokes at their expense.

And that damage, that judgement, causes real

issues in the world. In the first half of 2021, 1 in 4 queer teens attempted suicide. 25 percent of queer *children* took action to leave this world because they felt it would be better without their real selves. And we're kidding ourselves if we think that the church, the lack of acceptance, the lack of pride doesn't have anything to do with that.

We've got to do better. I'm determined to do better.

I know I'll never make up for the way I grew up believing, but I'm determined to spread as much love and acceptance as possible now. I hope you'll join me, whether it's with a Facebook post, a flag on your lawn, a shirt with a rainbow, a donation to a cause you believe in, or even passing this book on to someone else.

We all deserve to feel loved, exactly as we are.

ACKNOWLEDGMENTS

I'm so thankful I had the opportunity to write this book, and I couldn't have done it without all my readers who've supported the Curvy Girl Club and even requested a queer love story! This story is here thanks in large part to you!

My family has been so supportive in this journey, from my husband who's encouraged me and supported me along the way, to my boys who brainstorm titles with me, and my parents and siblings who help spread the word about my books! Love you all bunches!

My editor, Tricia Harden, is an incredible wordsmith but also a kind soul who always has supportive words to offer that speak to my heart. I'm so glad I could work with her on this story!

Najla Qamber, my cover designer, created the most beautiful, inspiring cover, and I am so happy to have it on the front of this story!

Several sensitivity readers helped me improve my representation of queer, hispanic, and black characters. Thank you Amiya Smith, Destany Tolbert, Mariam Perez, Alejandra Guadalupe Garcia, Caity Peaslee, and Abbey Haefner. I truly appreciate the care you put into this story to make it a safe place for more readers.

Sally Henson is my best writer friend, and I'm so thankful I have her encouragement along this author journey. It isn't always easy, but it's definitely not lonely, thanks to her friendship!

Judy Corry, Anne-Marie Meyer, and Laura Burton, thank you for your friendship and for helping me learn to better spread the word about my books!

And to you, sweet reader, I'm thankful for you. I hope you felt the love in every page.

ALSO BY KELSIE STELTING

The Curvy Girl Club

Curvy Girls Can't Date Quarterbacks

Curvy Girls Can't Date Billionaires

Curvy Girls Can't Date Cowboys

Curvy Girls Can't Date Bad Boys

Curvy Girls Can't Date Best Friends

Curvy Girls Can't Date Bullies

Curvy Girls Can't Dance

Curvy Girls Can't Date Soldiers

Curvy Girls Can't Date Princes

Curvy Girls Can't Date Rock Stars

Curvy Girls Can't Date Surfers

Curvy Girls Can't Date Curvy Girls (Pride Edition)

The Texas High Series

Chasing Skye

Becoming Skye

Loving Skye

Always Anika

New at Texas High

Abi and the Boy Next Door

Abi and the Boy Who Lied

Abi and the Boy She Loves

The Pen Pal Romance Series

Dear Adam

Fabio Vs. the Friend Zone

Sincerely Cinderella

The Sweet Water High Series: A Multi-Author Collaboration

Road Trip with the Enemy: A Sweet Standalone Romance

YA Contemporary Romance Anthologies

The Art of Taking Chances

Two More Days

Nonfiction

Raising the West

ABOUT THE AUTHOR

Kelsie Stelting is a body positive romance author who writes love stories with strong characters, deep feelings, and happy endings.

She currently lives in Colorado with her family. You can often find her writing, spending time with family, and soaking up too much sun wherever she can find it.

Visit www.kelsiestelting.com to get a free story and sign up for her readers' group!

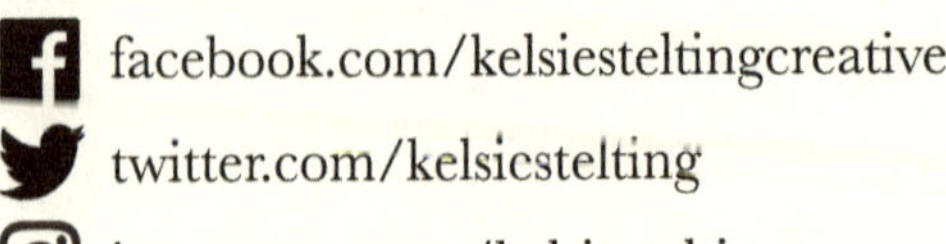

facebook.com/kelsiesteltingcreative
twitter.com/kelsicstelting
instagram.com/kelsiestelting